A. Montgomery

Pi

Stories

CATALOGUING IN PUBLICATION DATA (CANADA)

Burstyn, Irene, 1919-

    Picking up pearls

    ISBN 1-895854-71-7

       I. Title.

PS8553.U696P52 1997	C813'.54	C97-940477-0
PS9553.U696P52 1997		
PR9199.3.B87P52 1997		

Interested readers may wish to consult our ever-evolving catalogue
on the World-Wide-Web:
http://www.rdppub.com

Irene Burstyn

Picking Up Pearls
Stories of Nattie, Emily, Trudi, Lila and others

Robert Davies Publishing
MONTRÉAL–TORONTO–PARIS

Copyright © 1997, Irene Burstyn
Edited by Alexina Scott-Savage

Ordering information:
Robert Davies Publishing
311-4999 St. Catherine Street
Westmount, Québec, Canada H3Z 1T3

Telephone 1-800-481-2440
Fax 1-888-RDAVIES
e-mail: rdppub@vir.com

This is a work of fiction.
Names, characters, places and events are either
the product of the author's imagination
or are used entirely fictitiously.

The publisher wishes to thank the Canada Council for the Arts,
the Department of Canadian Heritage
and the Sodec for their generous aid to publishing programs
that helped make this book possible.

To Ignace

Table of Contents

Who is Irene 9
Nattie 11
Louisa 26
Maria Beàtricé 43
Emily 60
Ruth and Flora 73
Anna 78
Irka and Halka 83
Lady Penelope 92
Aline 95
Trudi 101
Three Ladies 111
Lila 141

Who is Irene?

During the heyday of haute couture in the 1950s and 60s, "Irene of Montreal" was a household name, synonymous with millinery chic. Irene Burstyn was *the* leading hat designer in Canada. Her creations were seen on the fashionable as they lunched at The Colony, took tea at the Ritz, cocktails at the "400" or dined at Café Martin. The hat was indispensable. And if your husband could afford it, it was created by Irene. Wearable Art, before the term became fashionable.

In 1944 Irene Burstyn arrived in Montreal with her husband and two year-old son, from Poland via Italy. In '48 she opened a modest studio on Mackay Street, in the centre of Montreal. After a few months she moved to 1522 Sherbrooke Street which became her permanent location for thirty years.

"Irene of Montreal", the name coined by *Weekend Magazine*'s Woman's Editor, Helen Gougeon, during their first interview, launched the boutique into the fashion world.

Twice a year Irene introduced Montreal to her collections, forecasting future trends with amazing and uncanny accuracy. Ahead of New York and Paris shows, Irene's creations were literally avant-garde and proved the designer's originality and fashion leadership.

The hats were worn by models dressed in black with hair invisible or pulled back into a tight chignon. Only the press were invited to these striking shows. Enormously helped by the work of her publicist, Enid Nemy (now with *The New York Times*), the shows were always an acclaimed success. Enid gave the hats whimsical names in her inimitably intelligent and witty style. The fashion elite flocked to her boutique.

Irene also accessorized other shows of The Fashion Group, especially those of Montreal's leading couturière, Marie-Paule Nolin. Irene's millinery styles were always dramatic and incisive, much like her writing style. She was invited to submit a design to update the headgear of the Order of Gray Nuns, gave lectures on fashion at Sir George Williams College and appeared on countless television programs.

With a clientele that at one time surpassed three thousand (something of a problem since the designer's card file cabinet could only hold this number), a workroom of five milliners under the direction of the première, Madame Basslier (who had previously trained with the leading Paris couturier, Paul Poiriet), realized the designer' creations.

Among Irene's internationally-known patrons were Jackie Desmarais, Jeanine Beaubien, Mrs. Saidye and Lucy Bronfman, Nelly McLean-Burke, Neri Bloomfield, many Mrs. Molsons, Margaret Trudeau and of course, Olive Diefenbaker, who would never appear in red, "only blue, Irene, we are conservatives." Mrs. Frank Ross of Vancouver, wife of then Lieutenant-Governor of British Colombia, was also a cherished client. Although Mrs. Ross purchased much of her clothing from European couturiers, including Worth of Paris, she always came to Irene for millinery. Mr. Ross frequently attended the sessions with the hat designer and would amuse himself by calculating the bill for the hat, including taxes, which he then addressed to himself! These clients, and all the others of Irene of Montreal knew that hats that were not "right" never left the atelier.

Twenty-five years later women still wear Irene's hats which are now classics. Her permanent public legacy remains with the McCord Museum in Montreal where eighteen hats, some of them surprisingly sculptural, tranquilly repose. Here we may see the consummate real thing! Included are no less than nine models designed for an avid fan, the diminutive Mrs. Jack Cole, who, according to legend, headed regularly towards Irene of Montreal when in need of sartorial or spiritual renewal!

And what of the designer today? Creativity always seeks an outlet and so, in a new career turn, Irene began to write, finding inspiration in all of her intense life experiences. This book of short fiction is the result.

Jacqueline Beaudoin-Ross
Curator of Costume and Textiles
McCord Museum of Canadian History

NATTIE

Tiny like a Dresden figurine. Barely five feet tall. Enormous black eyes. Masses of dark hair. Pretty. Coming down the airline steps, the heat hit her. With the first whiff of orange-blossom scented air, she knew. This is it. Walking the heat-softened tarmac, she was sure. This is for me. I love it. Here I'm going to live. I'll never go back to Poland.

And so she stayed. Guest of Dora, a school friend from back home. Dora was happily married. Settled with her curly-haired husband, Leo, in a tiny, uncomfortable apartment. Gone, pretty frocks. Gone, painted nails. Life was serious. Wife and husband both worked. Hard.

Dora, barely out of her teens, explained:

"Here there is no one to help. Here we have to make it by ourselves. This is the Promised Land, Palestine. Nothing comes easy. You get up at six in the morning latest, eat a huge breakfast, leave all windows closed and shuttered, and by seven you're at work. Lucky if you have a bicycle. For lunch, you come home, have a bite, lie down naked in the relative cool for siesta, doze the hottest hours away to be ready for the second part of your working day. Evening brings relief. Sundown. Work ends. A slight breeze from the sea wafts your sticky body. You shower. Feel cool. It's a good life," she said. "You'll love it." She giggled. "We love each other so much — make love at any moment we can snatch for ourselves. And you, Nattie, you too will find a good man. You'll be happy."

Nattie marveled how easily satisfied they were. Could she live this way? Work. Make love. Plan a distant future? No. That's not what she wanted.

In cafés lining white beaches on Hayarkon Street, under colorful umbrellas, toying with a cold drink, dreaming, looking at the pale, still sea, enjoying the heat like a lizard, she idled her days away. Observing animated people. Young. Suntanned. Well-dressed. Table hopping.

Obviously much at home. Leading a different life. How do they do it? If it is possible for them, will it be possible for me? How?

Walking along the boardwalk, she noticed smart villas. Flowers spilling over garden walls. Old Arab houses. Gracefully arched doorways and windows. Gardens overgrown with orange and lemon trees. She could almost feel the cool under low-hanging branches. She licked hot day's dust off her lips. Could almost taste chilled pomegranate juice. The sheer luxury of it — to lie on wicker in the shade, have a tall glass of frosted pomegranate juice served to her.

Nattie liked the café with a large terrace facing the beach best. Canopied in green, which made everything appear shimmery, dappled. Mysterious. Like under cool water. She became friendly with the Polish waiter.

"Who are those on the right of me? Those five men?" she indicated a round table. "I did not notice them here before."

"Oh, those? Arabs — wealthy Arabs. You are early today. Those guys eat lunch here every day. That's a reserved table. You see? They are waiting for me, they want to pay. We call them young bloods. Playboys." Removing the ashtray, he continued, "After lunch they go over to their club, race camels in the desert — do all sorts of interesting things — not like us Jews. They don't have to work. I have to run — will come back for your order."

Nattie saw the men get up, pocket their billfolds, saunter onto the street. In an instant she made up her mind. To follow. Curiosity and huntress-instinct propelled her. To see where their club is. Learn more. And they, after turning into this and that street, stopping on corners, leisurely, with friendly back-slapping, separated.

The one she liked best, the tall one, proceeded along. I'm lucky, she thought. And kept well behind him, not to be noticed. He went into a travel office. She hovered at a shop display. He left, after a while. She braced herself for action. Came so far, have to continue. Bravely entered the office. Girl behind the counter suggested trips, cruises, but Nattie, hesitant, pretended she could not decide. Then, inspired, asked the travel agent,

"You remember the young man who just left before I came in? He is a friend of my cousin. I know he has good taste, is he taking a cruise?"

"Oh, you mean Saïd Hanishave?"

"Yes, that's him."

Nattie went straight from the travel office to a luggage store. Bought the smartest suitcases, slightly perplexed how little money she had left over. But then, with youthful insouciance, shrugged her shoulders. Never mind. All or nothing. This whole trip is a gamble. Va banque.

Same evening, strolling along the beach with Dora and Leo, she casually mentioned her impulsive, sudden plan to take this cruise.

"If I'm staying here, and I know I am, before I take a job — seeing how hard both of you work, I feel like taking a vacation. Sort of a last fling of freedom. Only a few days, after which I promise! I will become serious! Will you miss me?" playfully asked.

"Yes, we will miss you..."

Embarkation was in Haifa. The boat scheduled to touch Beirut by way of Tyre, Biblos, Sidon. Nattie dressed carefully for the connecting bus trip: Tel Aviv to Haifa. Not by accident was her hair pulled tight into girlish braids. Not by chance did a white, demure collar frame her face. Big eyes innocently made up. Saïd must notice me. He must be intrigued by my appearance. He must notice me. While the boat slowly plowed its leisurely way north, Nattie plotted her next step. She did not need to. Opportunity presented itself right away. The Master of Ceremonies announced a get-acquainted party for the same afternoon.

Introductions were made at the entrance to the salon. Saïd was bored. Distracted. Looked around for the young girl with braids he noticed on the bus. She was nowhere to be seen. He wandered around without interest, almost ready to leave, when a pair of big eyes looked at him from under a fringe of bangs. The small head and heart-shaped face was not to be mistaken. It was the girl from the bus. Dressed for cocktails. Did not resemble herself of this morning.

During the usual "opening" chatter they found they both spoke French and English. They soon left the noisy salon. Went up to the top deck. He appraised her coolly. Carefully. Not too much décolletage. Good manners. Nothing brazen or vulgar. Yes, now he knew for sure that this little cruise, to look up the old Alma Mater in Beirut, was a good idea. Might even turn out very interesting.

And Nattie? She was in Heaven. Realized she had made a big impression. Found Saïd absolutely wonderful. Handsome. Attentive. Jeepers, she was falling for the guy! By nightfall, she found him irresistible. Hold on girl, she admonished herself, do not fall overboard!

But her fate was already decided. After Saïd arranged to have a table for two for the length of the cruise both their fates were sealed.

Her first candlelight dinner. He ordered wine. She noticed his hand pouring — so strong, so delicate. They talked about their childhoods. Nattie, half listening, longed for his hand on her skin. Imagined how it might feel. Scandalized, shuddered.

"Are you cold?" Saïd asked.

"No, I'm fine."

Her reverie passed. She smiled at the swiftness of its disappearance. And to herself: "Like hell I'm fine!"

"What are you smiling about, Nattie?"

He enjoyed the sound of her name. Wondered if her lips would feel as soft as they appeared. Pink rose petals. Would he kiss her tonight? No. He would not. Nattie was a gambler. She would hold onto her trump card. She shook her head while her eyes, full of promise, lingered on his. Her hand became limp in his grasp. And suddenly she was gone. Closed her cabin door softly. Proud of her strong will, determined not to succumb. She slept, flying in puffy white clouds, swimming in their surrendering airiness.

In his cabin, Saïd showered vigorously. "Yes, yes." He knew. He knew for sure. She felt exactly the way he did. She was as good as his. This bird was caught.

Next night, looking at the sky full of stars, he held her waist, nuzzled her neck. And she, shivering with delight and desire after his prolonged goodnight kiss, firmly but softly, closed her cabin door.

Time was a daisy chain with a tail of colored ribbons.

How was it possible for days to pass so quickly? Gratefully, she looked back at the boat gently bobbing on the cobalt sea. Waved it good-bye and insisted, for memory's sake, to take the bus back to Tel Aviv. Smiled away Saïd when he shook his head and laughingly suggested a taxi.

"But I can afford it!"

"I know, I know, but you did spot me first on the bus."

She caught herself batting her eyelashes at him. Felt ashamed because she had never before acted so girlishly. But then again, never before was she so bewildered by love.

They held hands on the bus. Like teenagers.

Back in the stuffy apartment she danced around while unpacking. Between the radio, the window, the sink where her things were soaking in soapy water. Why aren't they home yet? Impatiently, fiddled with the radio buttons. Music was too loud. Music was not loud enough. At last Dora and Leo came home. She hugged them passionately at the door.

"Hey, Nattie. Let us come in first! What is it? Let me look at you! What happened?"

"Oh, Dora, Dorale — I'm in love!!!"

Omitting entirely her own sleuthing role before meeting Saïd, fibbing here and there, she told her tale.

Both Dora and Leo sat across the kitchen table, round-eyed. Listening. Without making a comment. Till the end. Then Leo said,

"But Nattie, he is an Arab! Not only an Arab, but a member of one of the first and finest Shia families in the whole region! What would his family say? Listen girl, this is not for real. Forget it, it's impossible!"

Dora got up, took her aside, looked her in the face.

"Nat, did you sleep with him?"

"Of course I did not! I know enough not to spoil all my chances. No!! How can you even ask such a stupid question?"

They embraced, arms around each other's shoulders. They cried a little. Dora, from anxiety for her friend. Feeling somewhat responsible. Nattie, from happiness. Sure that she was on the right track.

"Don't cry, Dora, please don't cry. It's going to be alright for me. I know it!"

"How can you know it?" She wiped her eyes. "And what if you're left disappointed and hurt? You might blame me." She started to cry again. "Didn't I tell you you'd find a man and be happy?"

"Yes, you did. You said it, and I will be happy. You just watch me!" She blew her nose. "You just watch me!"

Leo went out to talk to their neighbors. He came back in a funny frame of mind.

"Nattie, you know what I found out? You probably don't need to know about it, but just in case. Seeing you are so sure this Saïd is serious about you, I found out there are three religions where the woman does not need to convert to Islam to be married to a Muhammadan. Three religions following scriptures: Jewish, Christian and Zoroastrian. Is that something? Well, I never ..." His voice trailed away. "Anyway, we do not need to worry about it. Not at all. It will all pass away."

But it did not.

The marriage was officiated by a Mullah. A simple affair. Nothing to it. A contract was drawn up. And duly signed.

"Nattie? You might not know it, but this contract, the one just signed? It stipulates that from now on I have the use of your body." Saïd smiled. Very smug.

And Nattie, overjoyed, laughed. "You have! You have!"

He continued, "Your body belongs to me."

Nattie, all asparkle, looking into his eyes, "I give you my body from now on until I die."

Her dream had come true.

To celebrate, Dora and Leo made a yard party. Big Sabine was there with her tiny husband, David. Saïd's childhood friend, Youssuf, and his Miriam. Bella, Sophie, Manny. All close friends.

The young couple moved into a small, gracious house in Jaffa. With a big garden. Just like the gardens Nattie admired and dreamed of owning when strolling along the boulevards of Tel Aviv. Surrounded by a crumbling old wall. The stones warm to touch. Her hand trailed the bark of an orange tree. She stooped under low-hanging branches of pomegranate. She pulled off a wrinkled, forgotten lemon from a lemon tree. This was all hers. The garden. The house. She murmured to herself, "I'm home, home ..."

She immediately started to wear the richly embroidered female robe, the thawb. Kohl-lined eyes looked into Saïd's face. Saw her husband was pleased. Very pleased. But no, she could not make him wear the traditional qubbaz.

"No, no, Nattie. I like the way I'm dressed."

The women employed in the house did a lot to educate Nattie. All the little ways a woman was supposed to endear herself to her spouse, all this was revealed to her. Smilingly. In whispers. In secret.

"You're not supposed to shave legs or private parts. Never. One uses hot sugar in this household, the Greek way. Some others use wax, like the Turks, but not here. One does it this way. Try, it's easy .... I'm born in a black tent — I'm a Bedouin." Raïsa with the hennaed hair added, "I hate the Turks."

Saïd was so good, so generous, so gracious, so tender, that Nattie almost forgot how painful the daily sexual act was for her. Being so very small, she had to brace herself with tightly clamped teeth for his love thrusts.

But never mind. She passionately loved her big, strong, satin-skinned spouse. And his teeth, his blue-white gorgeous teeth! Oh, how lucky she was!

The time was the Thirties.

Visitors coming from Poland dropped in to say hello. To be invited to lavish dinners on weekends. Just as it was supposed to be in a rich Arab's house. Hospitable. Freshly baked pita, torn to bite-sized bits doubled into scoops, dipped into fragrant, deliciously spicy delicacies. On an enormous platter in the middle of the table, the main dish — a saffron-scented, rice-filled, whole, roasted baby lamb. The room filled with the aroma of wild herbs and spices.

"Please, help yourself, help yourself ..."

The soft meat pink, cooked to perfection. Eaten daintily from the common platter. With three fingers of the right hand.

Nattie, beautiful, proud, covered with antique Bedouin jewelry. Showed off how good a hostess she could be to her Prince.

Sometimes, while the ladies stayed for a day of gossip, Saïd took their husbands hare-hunting. They drove out of town into a small Arab village and huddled on the sands behind a dune. Greeted effusively by the Muhtar, Saïd introduced his friends to the salaaming, broad-smiling Elders. An order flung out into the breeze brought out, on a run, three youngsters about twelve years old. Without ceremony they took away the three hunting rifles and with happy war cries, waving the rifles above tousled heads, scuttled towards the Vadi, their white shifts disappearing behind a dune.

In the Muhtar's house a feast was prepared. Carpets were scattered on the earthen floor. A crisp, white cloth placed in the middle. Little dishes of finest delicacies: humus, tahina, baba-ganoush, plates of dates, nuts, bowls of green and black olives scattered among hot pitas. Guests and hosts sat cross-legged around it. From behind the heavy, black felt curtain, among whispers and giggles, two women brought out the spit-roasted lamb. Faces covered, dressed in black, one could only guess at their age. Eating was done slowly, ceremoniously, with decorum. After the carcass of the roast was taken away, lemon water was passed around. To rinse off the three fingers. Spiced, hot coffee, black as night, followed. Served with golden honey cakes. To show full appreciation for the meal and hospitality of the hosts, there was unrestrained heavy burping and delicate patting of the full stomachs. At the open door the boys hovered, pushing, shoving, as boys will do. At the ready. Each departing guest was given back his rifle and a limp hare held aloft by long fuzzy ears.

At home, Nattie, with her Polish friends, invigorated, refreshed and relaxed, showed off her garden: freshly planted rose bushes and her orange, lemon, and pomegranate trees. She ended the day teaching them how to dance the Hora. On the grass.

Soon she became pregnant. Her youngest sister, Sylvie, came from Poland to stay. Officially, it was said, to help Nattie in her difficult times ahead. But gossip was rampant in "the Colony".

"Did you see? She sits on Saïd's lap all the time! Isn't he too playful with his sister-in-law? Nattie must have noticed it, for goodness sake! Of course she noticed it! She sees everything. I have a feeling this whole situation was worked out well in advance."

"What do you mean?"

"How would you like your husband to have a concubine?"

"What?"

"Yes. Yes."

"Or better still, a second wife? You know Saïd has the right to have four?"

"Don't even say it! Poor Nattie."

"Are you sure our men behave any differently? I mean the sleeping around with other females while their wives are big with child? Is that better? Oh, I don't know ..."

Saïd kissed her hands, her feet, her extended belly.

"It's going to be a boy. I feel it. I know it."

Nattie caressed his head.

"My beloved, I don't mind having the baby at home, but could I have a doctor in attendance — you know? In case of emergency. One never knows..."

"Yes, I thought about it — yes, of course. It will be arranged."

"Will it be a doctor from the Jewish hospital?"

"I knew you would want it that way. Yes. Yes. No need for you to fret ..."

When her time came the doctor arrived. The women of the household, resentful, shrugged shoulders, lifted eyebrows. Pouted when he insisted on white aprons and scrubbed hands. Under his orders in Arabic they quickly changed into efficient helpers.

It took hours. And hours.

At last. Utterly exhausted, Nattie was delivered of a big boy.

Saïd, jubilant, exhilarated. With tears in his eyes, praised Allah and thanked the doctor profusely.

"Nattie, my Nattie, now you are my rightful wife! You gave me a son! I have a son! You are to me like the stars in the firmament. Allah Akbar."

Nattie was barely able to open her eyelids. So very tired. She held onto the doctor's hand feebly.

"What will happen with the circumcision? What am I to do? It frightens me so ..."

He patted her hand.

"Do not feel anxious. They do it just as well as our Mohels. They have the same experience. Don't expect any emergency. But then you know I can be called. I assure you it will not be necessary."

And it was not. Nattie plugged her ears with tight fists not to hear the baby's wailing. Burrowed her head under pillows. And it passed.

The household settled to everyday living. The baby grew. Saïd was perpetually overjoyed when at home, which was not often. No one paid much attention to Sylvie now. She wondered what her mother was doing. News from Europe was ambiguous. Abruptly, she decided it was time to go home. Came to breakfast announcing her suitcase was packed. Expected some opposition. To Nattie's relief, none came from Saïd.

A big smile from him. "Sorry you're going. I expect mother needs you at home? It was good to have you here ... you will come again." And so on. Nattie hugged her sister. Gave her a pair of magnificent earrings. Saïd drove her to the airport. And that was that.

Saïd slipped into his old lifestyle. Friends, club, horses, camel racing. Full days. Outside his house there was his lively male world. Independent. A world into which Nattie had no entry.

World War II broke out. Little Sami was three years old. Some of Nattie's friends managed to reach Palestine. Tearfully embraced. Hugging for comfort. The Germans progressed victoriously, without hindrance. One might think: unbeatable. What was happening in Poland? Nobody knew for sure. Saïd listened to the evening news from Berlin. In Arabic. Exclusive news for the wide Arab world.

Still, life progressed at a seemingly normal pace. Saïd took special friends of his wife's to Jerusalem to meet his older brother, the V.I.P. of his important family. In the cool of the beautifully tiled hall, oriental carpets on black and white floor slabs, silent menservants dispensed English tea. In delicate cups.

Nattie stayed home.

He took them to his Tel Aviv club, at the beach, where they played with his little son, Sami.

Nattie stayed home.

They, in turn, took Saïd to Jeannette's, the famous fish restaurant, where Everybody met Everybody. He roamed the old Suk and the crooked narrow streets with them.

Nattie stayed home.

Her kohl-lined eyes wistful. Or so it seemed. She went out of doors only if accompanied by one of the household women.

Dora's close friends became Nattie's close friends. They spent evenings together discussing the world situation. Trying to interpret local happenings.

"Saïd, what will happen? What will happen if the war spills over here? Saïd, what do you think?" They kept asking him, "What do the Berlin broadcasts say in Arabic?"

Nattie, interrupting, "If something happens here, you girls come to me, I'll make Arab women out of you. I'll shelter you all."

After a pause, Dora interjected, "You met my cousin in Tel Aviv, Irene. The one managing the haberdashery, Adam's?"

"I know the shop! The most elegant and the most expensive! So, what about this Irene?" came from Big Sabine.

Did you know she was married to an Arab?

"No, I did not. I only knew she could recognize a Sulka tie from far across a room and I wondered who did her hair. It must be the best hairdresser in town."

"Her coup-de-vent ..." Mannie added, but was interrupted by Sabine.

"Same for her makeup — perfect! She is quite a looker."

"You can use the past tense. She is gone."

"What do you mean *gone*?"

"Just what I said. She is gone. Not here anymore. Vanished. Together with HIM."

"Why? Where?"

"Why? HE probably knew some things we do not. Where? One can speculate — I should think the logical place would be across the river to Jordan."

"What? You must be crazy! To Amman? What would she do there all alone? Poor soul, my heart bleeds for her."

Now Nattie added, "You all met Joseph, the one called Youssuf? The Palestinian Jew, Saïd's childhood playmate? His grandfather was Yaffo's mayor. This Youssuf even smokes a nargilla! One would never suspect him of being a Jew. Or his obedient wife, Miriam. Goodness me! Just like an Arab's wife. Just like me!"

She giggled. Looked at Saïd's somber face. "Don't mind me, my beloved," and continued, "their families live right here, in the same place, from biblical times — even they feel restless. Wondering ... Crusaders, Turks, British Mandate, and now what? Could something happen to them now? What? What could happen?"

Nattie was not a political person. Rumors and facts washed over her. But the news from Germany was most alarming. She did not know what or whom to believe. Palestine became a gathering point for Allied Forces: British, Australians, New Zealanders, Free French, Poles and a special Jewish Brigade. At last, Jews were allowed to bear arms in Palestine.

Nattie ventured with Dora into Tel Aviv. "You have to see what's going on," said Dora. "You won't believe it!"

And it was unbelievable. Everybody seemed to be out in the streets. From a sidewalk café they observed. Toothless young Aussies in unbuttoned army tunics. No belts. No hats. Where's Army etiquette? Careening down the street. Loudly singing, "Kiss me goodnight, Sergeant Major. Bring me to my little wooden bed ..." Some New Zealanders stopped an orange vendor. The Yemenite Jew ended with a fistful of money while the soldiers tipped over his wheelbarrow. Oranges cascaded down the width of Allenby Street towards the beach. From the passersby gales of laughter while the two Kiwis pushed their comrade into the wheelbarrow, his heavily booted feet waving in the air, the wheelbarrow almost tipping over. With whoops of laughter, the two soldiers pushed it down the street. Such scenes. Not to be believed.

Nattie was alone alot. Sometimes twice a day she lifted her head, listening. Heavy, ponderous drumming above. German Messerschmitts flying towards Egypt, heading towards Alexandria, where Rommel was holed up. Then later, again the wailing, warning sirens of Hazaka, when the same planes, having disgorged weapons and supplies to German troops, empty, headed home. Dreaded sounds. Frightening sounds. Hazaka. And the rasping voice of Jerusalem's Grand Mufti. Full of hatred. Forever sounding off on Arab radio against the Allies, egging on believers to rebellion.

Lately she looked at Said without words. Couldn't understand why he was not saying something? Anything! Should I ask? Better not. I'm not an Arab. He is getting farther away from me. Is it into the Arab world? The few precious friends keeping in touch with me, is that all I have? Why is my husband not at my side during these difficult days?

And Sami. He's taken Sami. My baby, Sami, doesn't he still need me? Oh, dear God in Heaven — is my world breaking up? This world is not my world anymore." Questions crowded her. "Was I asleep till now? Why didn't I see the truth? Why couldn't I have more babies? Would that have been better? Would Said have left Sami longer with me? No, I shouldn't fool myself. It would not have been the Arab way. Here, sons belong to Fathers.

Preoccupied with her inner loneliness she didn't notice when or how the war ended. Suddenly, Said came home, all excited. Called from the door. "The radio is not on, Nattie? Turn the radio on! War is finished. You did not hear?"

Before she could draw a breath of relief, grisly, horrible news seeped out of Poland. Ghastly. Shattering. Extermination camps. All her people murdered. The whole family. Everybody. Her sister, Sylvie. So good to her. So sweet. The enormity of it. Incomprehensible. Too much to absorb. Numbed with pain, she could not cry. Like a shadow she roamed the rooms. Dutifully attended to the needs of her home. Smoothed Saïd's life. Took care of growing Sami, now eleven, helping him with reading, homework. Now that his father looked after Sami's extracurricular hours: horseback riding lessons, watching camel races, having a lemonade with his father's male friends, again Nattie wondered, does he need me? No. He does not. Her smiles vanished. She wandered around the garden. Sat under the trees. And my husband, does he need me? Again, her answer was "No."

My home is here. I love it. My garden. Pomegranate, orange, lemon trees. Is that all? Bereaved, she wandered from window to window. Dry-eyed. Sometimes shaking off her dark mood. I should do something. I should go out. I'll get sick if I stay submerged in despair. What did Mother say? "Go out and do things." Urged me to take a dressmaking course, what else? "You have to be able to earn a living," she said. And I passed all exams brilliantly. Thank heaven I didn't need to work. I met Saïd. But mother said to stand on my own two feet. How do I do it? How? And what now?

The "now" gave her a jolt. An unbelievable, terrific jolt. Out of her Palestine, Israel was carved. There was much talk about it before it happened. Much speculation. Buzzing of theories. For years, promises. And now it happened! At last. Jews danced in the streets, drunk with joy.

From Jerusalem, the Grand Mufti raged over the radio.

"A bloody war is coming. A short, bloody war. Believers, go to Jordan. All of you. Go. Fight. The armies of our brethren will push the

Jews into the sea. Blood will be spilled. Jewish blood. After our victories you'll return to your land: plunder, rape, seek revenge and take back your homes."

That's what the Grand Mufti was preaching.

Nattie felt the ground shifting under her feet. Palestine was breaking up. Arab against Jew. Two peoples. Two cultures pulling apart. What could she do? Why hadn't she seen the rift coming? And what about her Saïd? Where would he stand? For or against her people? It used to be they were like one. Or did she imagine it? Was it love blinding her to their differences? The old feeling was gone forever — where was she now?

Completely bewildered, she longed, with all her inner being, for her family. She needed them. Now. Her sweet, soft Mother. Her dear Sylvie. Her supportive, wise Father. "Oh, come, help me, stand by me."

The only one who came was Saïd, running home. "Did you hear?" Violently banging the door, he shut off the radio's voice. "Enough! Enough!" he shouted. "Do you know what is going on in the streets?"

"Yes, the dancing ..."

"No, not the dancing! The megaphones! Army trucks roam the streets telling the Arabs to stay home. Blaring out: 'Stay home, nothing is going to happen to you! Do not run away! Stay home, stay home, don't run away!' That's what they say. Not I! I'll go!! You, Nattie, start packing. We are leaving."

"Leaving? Where are we going? You just said they tell us to stay home."

"Understand Nattie, I'm not taking any chances — we are leaving! Bloody Mufti! We're going to Amman."

"To Amman? Why?"

"Because we cannot stay here. My people are in Jordan. I have to go. You pack. I have to arrange things ... will be back shortly."

She wanted to say, "What about me?" but had no chance. Saïd was gone. Mechanically, she opened cupboards, drawers. First, she started to arrange Sami's clothing in a suitcase, then her own. Thinking, what about me? I just lost my whole family. My only friends are here. Should I submit and go to Amman with Said? I'll be completely dependant on my husband there. But for him, his family, his friends, in his land! No, this cannot be. I'll be all alone in an Arab sea. Mother said to stand on my own two feet. I will, I must take a chance at life.

In an instant, a decision. She called to the kitchen, "Raïsa, come up to help with the cases." Nobody answered. She looked in. All her help was gone. Dispersed. Gone. With resolve, she picked up the bulky case alone. Took Sami by his hand.

"Come, Son, we are going."

"Where?"

"You'll see."

"And Daddy?"

"He will come later. We have to go now."

She stood in front of her garden's gate and called to a passing urchin.

"See this money? You'll get all of it if you come back with a taxi for me — go!"

He left. A few minutes later he returned, standing on the running board of an ancient vehicle. With a whoop he tore the bills out of her hand and ran.

"You silly boy!" she shook her head, "I would have given you more."

The taxi driver lifted her case. She sat ramrod-straight in the back seat, holding on to her son's hand.

"Driver, straight on. Proceed to Tel Aviv, Mugrabi Center."

She did not look back. Did not want to see the ancient, gray wall of her garden. That's finished. No more, she thought. What will Saïd do when he reads my note? How could I have written it differently? How can one tell a husband, 'I'm leaving you', in words other than those naked, dry, painful words? Did he not leave me long before today? Way before?

She was last seen in Mugrabi Center, alighting from the taxi and standing with Sami next to the suitcase. Then afterwards — vanished! Traces erased. Where did they go? Right? Left? Nobody knew.

Saïd drove to Dora and Leo first. Found them jubilant in front of their apartment house. They looked into his eyes. Eyes wild with pain.

"What happened, Saïd?"

"No, Saïd, believe me, I'm her confidante, her best friend. I do not know where she went. She did not communicate with me. Yes, if she does. Yes. Immediately we shall let you know where she is. Yes, Sami. Your Sami. Useless for you to go to any of the others. If she did not tell us? If we do not know ... nobody will know. You're leaving? Leaving Israel? Don't go. Stay with us in Israel. Do not go, Saïd."

Long after the three Arab armies were repelled and vanquished, long after the thunder of fighting abated, long after the victory of the newborn state of Israel, Nattie wrote a long letter to Dora. Postmarked Canada. Swearing Dora to secrecy on the graves of her dead parents.

Nattie wrote: "Saïd is looking for me and for Sami all over the Middle East, Europe. I know he will come to you, Dora. If you have any feeling for me, don't tell him. If you tell it will be the death of me. Because he would take Sami away. Don't ever tell him, because I would die without Sami."

Saïd went again to Dora. It was easy for him to cross the Allenby Bridge on the Jordan, to move around the Tel Aviv he knew so well. Easy to find Dora and Leo again. He held on to Dora's hands. Cried. Begged her.

"No, no, no. I do not know where your wife is. Where your son is."

And she, herself, cried out of pity, seeing his pain. Both ended in each other's arms. But she did not tell.

He came again on a Sabbath, during a *Hamsin*. She sat with neighbours on the balcony trying to catch a breath of air. He "psssst" to her from behind the stone balustrade. Again, "Psssst." She realized who it was.

"Excuse me," she said to her guests and went out.

"Saïd, dear Saïd!"

He pushed a thick wad of money into her extended hand.

"Tell me! Tell me! You must know. Tell me! You must tell me!"

She did not. She pushed the money back into his hands.

"I don't know. I don't know."

She burst out crying. Returned to the balcony red-eyed.

"No, it was nothing. Nothing at all."

Montreal. Canada.

On a quiet street, in an elegant district, a man in overalls nailed a shiny brass plaque to the dark paneling of an entrance door.

Salon de Haute Couture.

LOUISA

From the back of the taxi, a slim, gloved hand reached out, paid the driver. There must have been a handsome *pourboire* for the man to jump out and hold the door open for her. She slowly got out, laboriously climbed the few steps. Before she touched the bell, the door opened. Her friend stood in the doorway beckoning her in with both hands.

"Come in, come in! Louisa, my dear girl, what happened? Why couldn't you tell me over the phone?" They embraced.

"I don't know. I'm so miserable. So distressed. But looking at you makes me feel stronger right away... that's why I felt I had to see you. I do feel better, now I'm here.." she said, stepping into the living room.

"Since my Max is gone it's you I count on. Forgive me. Forgive me for leaning on you, but I can't cope alone. I know I ask for too much." She stopped, hesitating.

"Don't be a ninny. You can cope! What am I saying? You DO cope. You're as strong as an ox. You do beautifully. Sit down. Here." Indicating a seat next to her on the sofa, comfortably tucking her legs under. "Now, tell me. What was it that upset you?" Both ladies sat facing each other. Lumped behind her was the light jacket Louisa shook off her slight, elegant body. She shuddered.

"Leave it here," she said. "I'm cold. I might need it."

"Alright, Louisa. Give me your hand. You're right. You are cold." Patting it lightly. "Let me warm you. A pot of tea?"

"No. No, Vivian. No tea. First I have to tell you. Oh, Vivian, it happened this morning. Terrible! I can hardly describe it. I got up to make a cup of coffee. When, passing the dining room, going towards the kitchen, in the big mirror — the one over the buffet, you know? — I saw a woman. Looking at me!" Louisa shuddered again. "She was looking directly at me. At first I did not know her at all. How did she get into my dining room? But when I came a step closer I seemed to remember seeing her. Somewhere. Where? I don't know. But I knew her for sure. Who was she? She still looked straight at me. It gave me a fright because she looked awfully familiar. How could I have forgotten this person? Oh, Viv, it was awful. It gave me a jolt. I shook. Could not move. And then, when I forced myself to take more steps and came up closer, I almost fainted, because this person in the mirror was me. Me! It took me a while to pull myself together to phone you and here I am. Vivian, my Viv, what came over me? What was this vision? Am I going crazy? Tell me! Help me!"

Vivian freed one hand to pat Louisa's shoulder comfortingly. "There... there. It was nothing. Nerves. Louisa, believe me, it was nerves. You're a very sensitive creature. First time alone in your entire life. Probably, you did not sleep too well during the night. Now, admit it, you didn't sleep well? You see? You were disheveled, did not like what you saw in the mirror — so what else is new? It was nothing. I assure you. Nothing. Now, I will make us a nice, strong cup of tea. You'll feel better right away."

"What would I do without you, Vivian? Such a friend! You're a Godsend!" She was almost consoled. "How is my make-up? Probably awful. And my hair?" She touched the French knot at the nape of her neck. "Undone. I'm a wreck."

It was a union made in heaven. Everybody said so. They were right. She —beautiful, blond, petite, blue-eyed, vivacious and very, very rich. And more. She was intelligent. Had a sense of humor. What about him? Not bad either. European education, great manners, a man of the world with many interests. And a first class lover. Financially well off. Nothing to compare with Louisa, but enough to establish himself in international business and hold his own in the clubs he belonged to. He played tennis. She, canasta. He had his meetings. She, her charity work. And so they lived a charmed life amidst a circle of equally charmed friends. Even their sex life was blessed. Married for years and still full of passion. Away from each other, busy with daily tasks, their minds dwelled on each other's bodies. Bodies known so well that they thrilled to scales, to adagios played mentally on their skins. Nightly sex was a concert leading to a crescendo. A passionate hymn of love. Truly it was a union made in heaven.

The War was but a pale memory. The Present was full of life's vigor. The Future was bright.

Louisa, splendid in peach chiffon, was a focal point at parties. Often, envious males — husbands of friends — followed the trailing coral gauze with hungry eyes. Sexy dame, they murmured. Nobody but nobody could wear apricot *mousseline de soie* like Louisa. It seemed to have been created for her blond beauty. Surrounded by other women's husbands she could trade off-color jokes. Asked no quarter. Gave none. Unembarrassed. Secure in the knowledge of her Max's protection in attendance across the brightly lit rooms.

Two girls were born in quick succession. A fabulous confirmation of their sybaritic life. Good, gentle, beautiful, well-behaved and adored by all. First, a perfect nanny took care of the perfect girls. Later, a private school took over. The sixties loomed on the horizon. Up to then all was well. Later there were small hints, only hints, mind you, of things to come. Rooms in complete disorder. Piano lessons abandoned. Strange music booming from under closed doors. Threatening. Cupboards full of discarded clothing. "Why didn't you put it in the hamper? This isn't even worn!" "I hate it," came the reply. Belligerent, strange behavior. Listening to parents was out. House rules — out. A different lifestyle took over. Dirt. Filth. Bodies and language were both filthy. The regular order of things, abandoned. Out. Washing — out. Charm — out.

"What do you want?" No answer.

Louisa wrung her hands. "What's happening? What did we do wrong? Was it me, or you, or both of us? Why? We gave them so much time... where did we fail? Breakfast together. Most dinners together. What's happening?"

The only one among her friends not touched by the sixties' calamity was her best friend, Vivian. "Thank God I didn't get married. Thank God I'm not a mother. Thank God."

"We have to do something, Max. Do something! For God's sake..." But Max, who could fix anything unpleasant in Louisa's life, could do nothing here.

"Let's talk," parents suggested. Reluctantly, the girls agreed.

But talk turned ugly. Violent. Precipitated a catastrophe: the girls moved out. With a toss of unkempt, long hair, with a shrug of contempt in their young shoulders, with derision in the swing of loose hips, they left. Packed blue jeans and shirts into rucksacks and were gone. Just like that, within an hour.

The house stood hollow. At night they both cried and made love out of pity for each other.

Friends' children moved into the basements of their big houses. Slept on floors. Refused to come up for meals. Only strange, terrible music with hostile words wafted upstairs.

News about them slowly leaked out. The older daughter moved in with a McGill social studies lecturer. The younger shaved her head, became an anarchist, apparently. At least, that's what she called herself.

In desperation, Louisa asked Max, "What can we do? What's there to do?"

Max was a good businessman. "Let's wait them out. They'll come back. Not now... later."

"How much later?"

"A year, maybe two... "

"I'll die before. My poor babies." cried Louisa.

"Wait, wait, be patient. We have to wait this deal out. Till their shoe-leather wears out. Till they miss good food, clean bathrooms. They will turn around. I'm sure," said Max. "They will."

She sat in front of a mirror inspecting her face minutely. I'm getting old, she thought. I can't deny it. I'm getting there. "No!" With rebellion, "I'm not!" Her index finger lightly touched the corner of her eyelid. Only laugh wrinkles around here. That's not getting old, is it? No. Touched her cheeks. Skin a wee bit thin here. Have to do something about it. But it doesn't mean I'm old. No. I'm getting middle-aged. Shook her head vigorously. Who am I trying to fool? How stupid can I get? I am middle-aged. And that's a fact. With disgust she turned away from the vanity's looking glass.

She made an appointment with her beautician, a touch-up with the hair colorist, and a manicure. As a matter of fact, the works. Can't allow myself to get down. Get depressed. Can't allow life to pass me by. And Max. Poor Max. Poor me. It's for him, poor lamb.

In the salon, she made an appointment for every consecutive Friday. Sometimes even for days in-between. "Have to take care of myself, she said to the manager."

She became very active at the golf club. Played almost every day. Vivian often came with her and read a book while Louisa went around the course. Those outings gave them a lovely time: fresh country air, lunch undisturbed under a striped umbrella. Relaxing.

"Such an attentive service," said Vivian. "I love it here. You know, I see how you carry this weight on your shoulders. I guess being a mother is a lifetime sentence without reprieve for good behavior. Each time you talk about the girls I'm grateful to fate for not ever having to listen to the "patter of little feet". Sure, it takes all kinds... do you hear from them? Do they at least phone?"

"I can't lie, Vivian. Yes, we did hear once from the girls. Do you notice how time passes without us realizing it? Unobtrusive... a year passed. A year! They called. For Father's birthday. Kind of them, wasn't it? Mine, they conveniently forgot. Never mind. Who knows? We might hear from them again before the second year is out. Look, the important thing is, they're well."

"No need to pretend, Louisa. I know what you mean. And it's much more than just mere health. Being well is not all. But as you say, never mind..."

Events did not stay put. Things did happen. The following year, Marion, the older girl, phoned. No birthday imminent. No excuse needed. She was hardly able to hold back the sound of weeping.

"Mom, I'm pregnant. What do I do?"

"Over the phone? You want me to give you advice over the phone! After an absence of nearly three years? Are you mad? Come home. Sit down with us. With me and Father. We shall talk. We'll see."

She did come. Defying them and crying at the same time. "This pregnancy was not planned," came out between sobs.

"I should hope not!" from Louisa. "So, now, the time's ripe for you to decide. Do you want OUT of this relationship? Fine — we'll send you to Switzerland. You'll come back whole again. No more talk about babies. You'll go back to school. Start from the beginning. We shall help you to pick up the pieces. Or, if you love your young man, bring him home. Let's see this wonder of wonders. If all goes well have a quiet wedding at City Hall. You'll start a new life with the baby. A normal life. Like other people have. As I said, if all goes well, we might even help. You decide ..."

The next day, in a conversation with her friend:

"Don't be naïve, Viv. How else could she have decided? Of course she's going to have the child! And you know, the lecturer, her young man, is not half as bad as we thought. So, my Vivian, can you imagine me as a Grandmother?"

"Oh, don't be surprised, Louisa, I can see you very well. Only don't overdo it. Please take it lightly. If you only could take it lightly..."

"Yes. I can. The girls taught me a lesson. I learn well. I'm going to think first and foremost about us. Me and Max. Maggy and Marion are not little girls anymore. Their criteria are not mine or Max's. No!

No more of this terrible pain and gloom! No more longing for love! For their mere presence! Now, it's me and Max only."

Then later, much later, events took over. Again. A call from a doctor about their younger daughter, Maggy. In the hospital with infectious hepatitis.

"The worst is over," said the doctor, "but I would suggest you come here and speak to her. She would do better with the proper rest and good food one can only get at home. The life she leads now is not very conducive to a speedy recovery."

And to Vivian: "Dear heart, do you see? You see how impossible my life has become? This calamity! Maggy, my little baby... so sick..."

But once the "baby" was home it was not easy. Not easy at all. Between bouts of gratefulness —depression. Then a terrible resentment bubbled up. Alienation.

"What is it, Maggy? Tell me! What is it I can do?"

"No, Mother. You can't do anything. It's life. That's all. Life." At least her hair grew back and she looked almost normal. Sickly yellow. Thin as a waif. But normal.

About that time it was decided enough is enough. The moment she gets well and moves out again the house will go on the market. "We don't need a house," they told each other. The girls were gone. Gone for good. Gone from Louisa's mind as well was the idea of weddings. Beautiful weddings with maids of honor. With bridesmaids. Orchestras. She, the queen of the event. Mother of the princess-brides. The heirloom veil, long in the family, repaired again. The silken web's tears sewn up with blond human hair threaded through the finest needle obtainable. Gone from Louisa's mind was the table laden with presents. Flower arrangements ... place cards ... thank-you notes .... It's never going to be. The joy. The laughter. Tearful good-byes when they left home for honeymoons ... never ... never ... never ...

They started actively looking around. Where to move after the prospective sale of the house? Found a rental suiting them to a "T" in a most prestigious condominium building. The one where Louisa already felt very much at home. Where her hairdressing salon was located. Where she knew the shops. What's more important, the dress shop owner, the shoe salon clerk, the bathroom boutique staff, they all knew her. Was accustomed to lunch with friends in the building's cafeteria. Years and years *habitué*, Louisa would not even miss the old house. This new place was so very convenient, so well known, and so near Max's office.

Looking in the mirror, Louisa felt consoled. Wrinkles still here but, I'm okay, I feel good. Smiled at her own reflection. "Mirror, mirror on the wall ..." I know what brought it on. Why I'm feeling better. The beauty salon, combined with my feeling of having done all that's possible is what did it. Marion's almost happy with the lavish layette plus a monthly stipend. The baby girl, a picture of sweetness. Maggy? Maggy's not happy at all. Alright, let her go to Europe. It might be this is what she needs. With this daughter of mine I do not know what's right and what's wrong. And that friend she lives with! I cannot accept this strange woman. The way she looks, with this orange hair, hanging on to Maggy. I warned her. I said, "Maggy, your allowance is all you can count on. Better learn to manage ..."

Before the sale of the house was finalized Maggy came home again. Dear God in heaven, what ails this girl? Louisa thought, let it be the last time. Let it be the last confusion. Thank God, it was.

The house was sold. Both young women picked over the furniture. Took what struck their fancy. The rest that was not needed for the condo was sold, given to charity, or to friends' children. Louisa, with the professional help of an interior decorator, furnished her new abode absolutely perfectly. The beautiful pieces stood out better here than in the old house. There was so much more light, space, air, here. It took them a few weeks to find their footing. Where is this? Where is that? But after this short period it was fine. Louisa was happy. Adjusted. Felt this was the right spot to wake up to in the morning.

The party, as always, was quite lovely. Guests were placed at candlelit tables for six. A lavish buffet was set amidst colorful flower arrangements, followed by a board of mouthwatering, exotic desserts. A lady at the piano played golden oldies for dancing. Everybody had some turns on the floor. Louisa, ravishing in peach silk. Max, distinguished and handsome in his tuxedo. They ate sparingly. Drank moderately. Gossiped amidst bursts of laughter, like the others, about everybody on the premises. And, replete with *bonhomie*, left for home about midnight.

As was the habit lately Louisa woke up to go to the bathroom. Coming back to bed she looked, in passing, at the little marble clock on her vanity. In the dim night light she could barely discern the hour. 3:30. Cold, she shivered. Her feet were cold. She quickly climbed back into bed. To cuddle. Have to cuddle close to him. His feet are always warm. My Max, he is warm even in the middle of winter. Her feet sought his. Her belly touched his hip.

"Oh my God Oh my God Oh my God!" She cried out.

His body was ice cold. Like a shot she turned away. Snapped on the bedside lamp. Sat up. Looked at his face. Her Max's face. With an open mouth, with a shriek plugged in her throat, with a leaden, dead-weight stomach, unable to suck in air for a breath, she looked at the white-gray sunken face of her husband.

Louisa lay on the sofa in the spare bedroom. Eyes closed. Covered with a warm shawl. The last words she spoke were the day before when she gave the voice at 911 her address. Since then not a word. Not even to her daughters. Was she dozing? Sleeping? Who knows? Max's friends phoned the newspapers. Made all arrangements. Vivian hovered around the apartment, forcing Louisa to take some tea, to bite into toast. She was there day and night. Louisa felt her presence, knew she was at hand, and opened her mouth once to ask a favor: "Buy black crêpe for me. A large square, please. When burying my husband I don't want people to read my face. To read my pain. To see me."

It was a large funeral. Their whole social circle. Max's business friends. Associates. Members of clubs they belonged to. Even casual acquaintances came. A large funeral. Louisa, shrouded in black crêpe, pale as a ghost and shaky, wobbled on her legs. Supported by Marion and Maggy at the rim of the swamp-smelling dank, wet, hole.

Soon mourners dispersed. Close friends remained to follow the family home for refreshments. Once inside the door Louisa disappeared into the spare bedroom. Her sofa. Her shawl. She remained curled up for the rest of the day. And for the following days.

Days turned into weeks. Sometimes she ate some cheese or whatever was handy in the fridge. It could have been the middle of the night. Or any other haphazard time of day. Vivian dropped in every day. Tried to talk her into getting up. Into resuming a semblance of life. It was futile. Louisa looked at her, turned away and resumed her huddled-up position on the sofa. Weeks later, Vivian decided that it was time to do something drastic. She shook Louisa's shoulder vigorously.

"Listen, Louisa, for goodness sake, listen. You cannot remain like this any longer. It's enough. You've mourned enough. You look grubby. You smell grubby. It's not like you at all. Look at me! And don't give me this "face" anymore. It won't work. I've decided, if I come tomorrow at this time and you're not up and about I'm going to turn on my heel and leave. Leave for good. And I mean it! Because you'll be telling me that you do not need a friend — you need a shawl, a sofa and a slow death. And I do not want to be witness to the suicide of my friend. So, I'll go away."

After a while, Louisa roused herself. Got up. Looked into the fridge. Found eggs. Made an omelet. Went to the phone to call her cleaning lady she'd told weeks ago not to come till further notice.

"Please come tomorrow."

She took a long, hot shower, changed into a fresh pair of slacks and a clean blouse. And that's how Vivian found her. Wan, pale. But back among the living.

"Come with me to the bedroom," she said. "I haven't gone in there yet."

Stood at the threshold. Looked at the mirror across from the bed. The mirror where their bodies had been multiplied a million times. Their entwined limbs almost engraved onto the surface. Only for her to see. She grabbed a small chair near at hand and, with one strong swing, smashed it into the glass. She was too quick for Vivian to make a move to stop her. Shards sprayed — flew onto the carpet. The chair fell out of her grasp. It happened in a flash. It was done.

The erasure.

The cleaning lady's flop-flop of padded feet stopped at the door.

"What happened?" she asked, frightened, turning her head from one woman to the other.

"Oh, never mind. It was an accident. Bring the trash can to pick up the pieces," said Vivian.

And when she left at a trot towards the kitchen Louisa grabbed Vivian by her shoulders. With clenched teeth, spewed her anger. "He had no right! No right to leave me alone! He promised! No right to leave me like this!"

The cleaning woman stood round-eyed at the door, the broom and scuttle in her hands. Her presence put a stop to Louisa's outburst. Rage unspent, she almost collapsed, knees weak, face in tears, at Vivian's breast.

"Why? Why?" she cried.

After a bite of cold supper in the breakfast nook they had a friend-to-friend talk. One-sided. Only Vivian spoke.

"Louisa, you have to take care of yourself. It's either-or. No suicide means you choose life. And life is to do things. To become interested again in each day. Look at yourself — it's not you at all!"

In the end Louisa could only add, "You're right."

She slept badly. Tossed. Turned. Mulling all arguments back and forth. Thought in the end, she's right, have to pull myself together. Starting with me. As in capital "I." Let's see ... and looked in the mirror. "Goodness, what a sight!"

Phoned downstairs to the Salon and spoke to the manager.

"Oh yes. We know of your tragedy. Our heartfelt condolences. We missed you.... Yes, of course. The staff will understand. Not a word. Absolutely. Nobody'll mention your absence. Just as if nothing's happened. It's been only a few weeks. Sure, it will be taken care of. And again, my condolences."

Should I look into his cupboard? No. I can't. Not yet. Will ask Vivian. Or better still, one of my girls. Yes, Marion. I'll ask her.

"Marion, I need your help. Phone the Salvation Army to take out Max's stuff. All of it. They can do it while I'm downstairs. No, Marion, for nothing in the world will I look on while his cupboard and drawers are being emptied out. No. I'll spare myself that additional pain."

Max, Max, what did you do to me?

And there by the phone on the small table she rested her head in both arms. Cried bitterly.

In the upper part of the Salon she had "the works". Body massage, colouring, facial, manicure, pedicure. Went down to the lower level for hairdressing. Exhausted, completely done in, she dragged herself to the elevators for home. Laid down. Once more the sofa. For God's sake, what am I going to do? Fell asleep. Wondered later, how come I fell asleep? Miraculous...

Spoke to her daughters. Both were eager to see her, to come over. But, no, she told them:

"Just wanted to let you know I'm better. Go on as you were. No, I'll take care of myself. Yes, maybe on the weekend you'll come for lunch. Just you two, okay? I want to see you."

And so she slowly crept into her old routine. Bored. Sad. And cold at night. The new mattress felt just that — new. She hardly recognized her bedroom without the large mirror. Strange. How it changed! Like a new room. Now she slept here alone. Her clothing roomed in both wardrobes. Lots of empty space. Still. Empty. Empty as her nights.

Wandered around the apartment. What am I looking for? Am I still searching for Max? I don't want to do it! He's gone, gone. It's finished!! Furious, she opened a drawer in the bureau. "Nothing here." Shut it with a bang. Opened the next one. Found a pen. His pen. Max's old fountain pen. The one he stopped using years ago. Threw it to the floor. Banged the drawer shut. In the bottom one, in the corner, his old billfold. Bought for an anniversary so long ago. "It's a million years old. I don't want it here!" Slapped it to the floor. And now, enraged with pain, face drenched with tears, ran from room to room, from cupboard to cupboard, frantically getting rid of any tangible remnant of Max. "This belt, how come it's here? Go!! Go!! Max is here no more — go!!"

The belt, pen, and billfold on the floor made her uneasy. She gingerly put them into a plastic bag and with determination pushed it down the trash chute.

To organize her thoughts she went for a long walk. Dialogued with herself.

"Don't rely on your girls. They have their own lives. Do I want to be part of it? No. So, I have to distance myself. And Vivian. Such a perfect person. I have to try to let her go as well. Not to give up this friendship — I could never do that — and why should I? No. But I have to try to be myself. How? How? I will find a way... I have to...."

Phoned the "canasta girls". Went to the club with some. Took bridge lessons. Still, her nights were frightfully lonesome. And cold.

Maggy's departure day for Europe approached. Met her, *tête-à-tête*.

"Don't forget, Maggy, I'll always be here for you. Don't allow people to live off you, to hang on to you. This will slow you down. And that's no good. Like the woman you share the flat with..."

"But Ma, she's my friend. Don't you understand? We live together! We're together."

"What? How stupid can I be? Dear heavens! I did not understand. You are a lesbian? Well, as my Mother used to say, live and learn." She paused. "Still, you're my daughter. I love you. Nothing can change that fact of life. But I never... never... difficult to get over it — to adjust. But my dear Maggy, I don't feel any different towards you. I feel strange but not awkward. You're still my Maggy. Only, poor you, poor me, how life turns out to be — give me the word — I have no word to describe it — yes — unpredictable, that's the word. Well. We both grew up. We're not the same women we were years ago. God keep you."

Taking care of face and body became Louisa's anchor. Kept her on an even keel. Each session at the Salon relaxed her. Made her feel alive. Younger. Centered all thought on herself. Is it good? Is it bad? She did not know. And did not care. Whom do I punish with this extravagance? Thank you, Max. You made it possible for me with your clever financial investments. You were such a gentleman. To the very end. A gentleman. Could have lingered in a hospital bed. But no, you made it easy for me. Painful like hell — but easy.

At the hairdresser she looked around. Young customers abounded. Attentive young people served them. Elaborate gestures. Fussy. Pampering. Women love it. I love it. Looked at the hairdresser in the mirror. Not at herself. Did not see herself. How odd! Can't see my face. She looked at the young man standing behind her, fluffing out her hair. What a doll! Gee, some doll! She now noticed three top shirt buttons open. Showing his chest. Showing everybody his smooth, bronzing-salon-tanned chest. And the gold medal. I wonder who gave it to him? Is he gay? No. Did he not tell me he has a girlfriend? Yes he did. Both putting away money for their own establishment. Smart kid, Alex. I'll ask him about the others. At least I'm sure his name is Alex.

"Are your parents Russian? — because of your name — a very nice name. Isn't it Sasha? Yes, I knew it was Sasha. The other one on your left, he is Rusty? Such pretty, curly hair. He looks like a gypsy. He sometimes dresses my hair. Are you friends? The new one, the blond one, his name is Alfie, isn't it? Good looking, too. The tall one, he's never attended to me. What's his name? Gordon? Sometimes when you guys are busy aren't there two more who come only for weekends?"

She went home quite animated, an idea brewing in her mind, her thoughts dwelling on bodies of young men. Displaying themselves for her. Weren't they? Of course they were.

Hey, what's going on with me? Nothing is going on with me! I'm conscious of their sexy bodies, that's all. And why not? If men can, why can't I? Indeed, why not? Why can't I? Nice bodies. Slim hips. Flat stomachs. Tight buttocks clad in blue jeans. Loose khakis. Denims. Freshly pressed. Neat. Clean. All open-shirted. Very nice.

After a day or two, Louisa broke a nail. Had to go downstairs to have it fixed. Looked around some more, making up her mind. How to proceed. What to do next. Her usual day of appointment was Friday. "So soon ..." She made a plan. First of all she phoned Vivian.

"Viv, I'm sorry, but I can't make it on Saturday night. No, it's one of the *canasta* girls. You don't know her. Asked me to interview somebody for a job. So, I'll stay home. How about meeting Sunday? We can take in a movie? You don't mind? Sure. I'm sorry, but this girl thinks

I have more experience in household affairs.. being older... and so on ..."

Am I going to go through with this plan? How do I know it will work? Or I might get cold feet. So many things can happen... but have to be prepared. In case it works out, Saturday has to be free.

That was the Friday she got up early and took the car to St. Denis Street. She'd never shopped in this district before. With dark glasses and kerchiefed hair, nobody would recognize her. Soon she found what she was looking for. *Lingerie Elegante.*

"I'm looking for a satin peignoir and nightgown. Preferably peach or pale salmon. No, not red, it's vulgar. Yes, this will do beautifully. Her fingers ran over the slinky material. Could you fix me up with bed sheets and pillow cases? Yes, the same material. I understand that this is not a factory production. This was done locally by somebody. Could you inquire from this person? Maybe phone? I would be grateful. I'll wait. While you're at it, could you ask if it could be finished for tomorrow?"

She did not hear what was spoken over the phone, but the smiling face said it all.

"That's fine. I don't mind the price since I'm in such a hurry. It's a gift for a dear friend. I'll come around then in the afternoon."

With her spirits high and a flutter in her belly, she looked around at the hairdressers. I'll try Rusty she thought. What do I risk? Nothing.

Paid her bill. Turned to leave, then, like an afterthought, she came back. Addressed Rusty.

"Would you have some free time tomorrow? After work? My hair will need combing. I'll make it worth your while. Oh, that's fine. I'll treat you to a glass of wine as well." And with a smile — left.

Saturday afternoon she came back from St. Denis Street with her parcel. Quickly changed sheets. Pillowcases. Fixed candles. Passing the dining room mirror, she glanced at herself. Pursed lips said I don't like you. Was it her face she did not like? Was it what she saw in the mirror she did not like? Is that me? That's not me. Face faded before her very eyes. It's the mirror. Can't stand it. It mocks me. "Don't mock me," she said aloud.

Hateful mirror. She proceeded to the kitchen. Avoided looking into it when coming back with wine bottle, glasses, corkscrew. Head turned away. "To hell with you," she said. Hastily undressed. Perfumed her body. In the oncoming dusk she slipped on the new finery, skin thrilling to the touch of the fabric. Looked at the apparition in the pier glass. Is that me? I look like a *cocotte*! With a shrug, turned the mirror away from herself. So what?

Fragrant and ready. Way before the Salon's closing time. Need to steady my nerves. My stomach's in a flutter. She poured ruby-red wine into a glass. Slowly sipped. And when the chimes sounded, she went to open the door with determined, steady steps.

Looked into Rusty's eyes. I wonder. Does he read me? Yes. He does. Rusty took in at a glance her trailing satins. Imperceptibly lifted an eyebrow, she noticed, like in the movies. She almost giggled nervously. Yes, he knew all right. Smart kid. She extended a hand with a fluffy white bathrobe. Pointed to the bathroom door.

"In there. In there you can take a hot shower. I'll be in the bedroom." For goodness sake, I've done it!

Bedroom lights off. A mass of candles banked on her vanity. Reflected in the mirror. It's so obvious, she thought. But so it is. Why should it not be? Light glimmered — soft. Flickering. Golden.

He entered, wrapped in the large robe. She, smilingly, pointed to a wine-filled goblet. "Here, have some wine. And take off your robe."

He stood naked. Gorgeous. Her mouth suddenly filled with saliva. She had to swallow, slowly. Hoped Rusty didn't notice. Embarrassing. But he didn't. She looked, with a tickle in her throat. The tickle turned into a smile. How funny.

"My, Rusty! You are a redhead! Now I see why the name Rusty suits you so well." She languidly extended her arm towards the young man with the wet, gypsy-black curls on his forehead.

He left three hours later. The two one-hundred dollar bills, sealed in an envelope, slipped into his jacket pocket.

"Would you come here again?"

"Sure! Why not..."

She slept dreamlessly. All night. Woke up vibrantly alive. Fresh. Young.

Felt like singing. Wow, wow ...

Monday, immediately after breakfast, she went again to St. Denis Street. Into *Lingerie Elegante.*

"My friend was very happy with the gift." Her eyes behind dark glasses avoided the glance of the woman behind the counter.

"She asked me to order two more sets. Not satin. Something chiffony with ruffles? Candy pink will do fine. I like this color. And this other one, too. The pale one. Can you find matching color satin for sheets and pillows? I rely on your taste. Maybe more ruffles? Right along the edge of the wrap? Oh, just this way, is it possible? I like it."

Wednesday night Louisa found sleep impossible. Close to 3 a.m. and she still tossed and turned on hot sheets. Could be I'm hungry — have to eat something. Went through the dining room.

The mirror. Can't see. It's dark. Light enough, but I can't see my face. My face is gone from the mirror. She shivered. Oh, imagination. It's crazy. I'm hungry, that's all.

In the kitchen she stood at the counter and, with bare fingers, gorged herself on cold chicken. And bread. And pickles. Some more chicken. Still hungry. My gut's full and I can't fill up. She knew then that it wasn't food she craved. Back in bed —images of bare men's bodies. Mercifully, she fell into oblivion, slept.

And so it started. Louisa's obsession with sex. She could not have enough sex. The routine already established, only her excuses to Vivian changed. Could not stand the thought of losing her Vivian. Have to keep her as my friend. But what about the people around her? The others? She was very careful with her acquaintances. That, she was sure of. At the Salon it was more difficult. Especially because, to keep her appetite sharp, she now alternated Rusty with Alex. I'm getting crazy! People will start to notice. And the two men? Surely they talk between themselves. I'm scared. How long? How long will it be a secret?

Poor Louisa, it was not a secret anymore. She didn't see the snickers. Here. There. She did not hear the off-color remarks. "A nympho!" And worse. The staff talked. What worried her was, that with the money lavished on her lovers, she might become redundant. She might bore them. She might tire them in her obsession. Money will lose it's importance, its appeal. It will be over. What will I do? Dear God in heaven, what will I do? Oh, Max ... Max ... it has nothing to do with you. With my love for you! This is just sex. I love *you*. Please forgive me. I'll love you forever.

Dates of weeks, months, lost their importance. She lived from one night with Alex to the other night with Rusty. In the meantime she went through the everyday motions. Lunched with the daughter of a friend. Played cards. Did marketing. All those functions 'on the side.' Just let them pass. Let there again be a night with a young male body. Hot-shower-humid. Limbs tired amid crumpled sheets. Legs. Legs this way. Arms that way. The golden lassitude. Hair tangled on silken pillows. Eyelids heavy with satisfied sex-hunger. Barely able to see the young man pull on his pants. Or struggle with a still-buttoned shirt, torn off his chest a few hours before by her own eager fingers.

"Will you come again?" whispered.

"Sure, why not?" nonchalant reply.

Let it go on and on and on. Let it never end.

While getting ready for evening encounters, she avoided the dining room mirror.

I hate that bloody piece of glass! It shows ME. Why can't I stand the way I look? It's sheer nonsense. It's my mirror. I can take it off the wall. I can phone the concierge and have it removed right this minute. Why then don't I do it? What stops me? And why don't I like what I see in it? How come I don't like ME? My face is only slightly made-up. Blond hair loose around my neck. What's wrong with all that? It's all silliness! One day I'll do it! I'll have it off the wall. It's only glass ...

In the meantime, passing back and forth, she kept her head averted. Looked the other way. And did not like herself for it. Musing. It happened before. Why does the mirror blank out on me? Something is wrong with the mirror or the light or maybe both. Or is it my imagination?

It was a Friday like other Fridays. Alex finished fluffing her fine hair. Talked. Like always. About the weather. Florida. A new dish he cooked for his friends last Sunday. And then, out of the blue, he said something which hit her. Like a thunderbolt. Suddenly she felt limp. About to faint. Ringing in her ears. A tremor in all her limbs. What did he say? He said something she did not want to hear. But hear it she must. Pull yourself together, Louisa. She shook her head from side to side.

"What did you say, Alex?" in an almost inaudible whisper.

"I can't come tomorrow," he repeated. "My girlfriend discovered weeks ago what I was doing on Saturday evenings. I explained. I said, it's business. I said, it's money. Money for our Salon. I told her it has nothing to do with my feelings for her. She then allowed it. "Okay," she said. "Yes. Go to her. But one day, soon, it will have to stop." Today she told me, "Stop it now." Sorry. I liked to 'visit' with you. I can't do it anymore. You do understand?"

She listened. She heard every single word. But hardly could make any sense out of it. What she understood plainly, distinctly, was — it's over. This was the end. The end with Alex. Rusty! For God's sake, there's still Rusty! Maybe he'll stay in my life. God, make it so! Let Rusty keep coming to me ... but her limbs trembled. Ringing in the ears persisted.

The mirror in front of her blanked out. It had happened before. Why does it do this to me? It must be the light. A trick of light.

She paid her bill at the desk. Did not speak to Rusty. I'm afraid. I might hear something I don't want to hear ... there is still hope .. and maybe some other young man ... there is still hope ... have to have faith ... have to stand tall. Keep up appearances. My hair... my body ... there will be others...

At home she had a double whisky. Fell asleep on the sofa. Woke up after two in the morning. What time is it? Where am I? Why am I here? And she remembered. Got up. Took off her clothes. Washed and creamed her face and slumped down in bed, only to turn feverishly from side to side. Probably slept but was not conscious of it. Late daylight coming through the venetian slats woke her up. Still was not sure she had slept. What she was sure of was that she was sick. Sick with something.

Got up unwillingly. Practically pushed herself up from the sheets. Slowly went towards the kitchen for a drink. Maybe coffee? Maybe juice? She did not know. Was terribly thirsty. Max, forgive me. I love you. I'll love you forever. This was only sex. You spoiled me. You were too good. Forgive me. The life you filled so thoroughly, so passionately, I miss. I can't do without it.

Passing through the dining room, she had no strength to avoid the mirror. And she saw this... this face. This person was there in it...

Vivian I need you. Vivian! Hastily, as hastily as her body would allow it, she dressed. Her mind going round in circles. Have to go to her for help. Have to go.... She felt desperate. Viv is sane. She will know. Will know what all this means. She'll help.

Called a taxi.

Tell her? Tell Vivian? Never will I tell her what's going on in my life. It's private. Secret. To stay with me. Me. And only me.

From the back of the taxi her slim, gloved hand reached out. Paid the driver. Got out slowly, the driver holding the door for her. Was hesitant.

However am I going to climb those stairs?

She saw Vivian through the living room picture window. Waving to her.

Went quickly towards the entrance. To open the door.

MARIA BEÀTRICÉ

A finger wanders around the map of Europe. Where does it stop? Somewhere warm. Like the shores of the Mediterranean. But not France or Italy. Why? Too big. And Monaco will not do either. Too touristy. That leaves Spain or Portugal. A strip of tired land breasting the Atlantic. Oldworldly. Sophisticated. Deliciously decadent.

I

Portugal. That's where the girl was born. As a newborn — quite ordinary. A healthy child. No more. Not one of those fat, jolly babies one longs to hug and kiss. The ones with rosy cheeks. No. This one was ivory white. Huge eyes. Astonishingly small, flat ears. Thin, delicately flaring nostrils in an otherwise formless nose.

Heads bend over the bassinet. Admiring whispers.

"What a beauty."

"Don't you think she resembles Grandmother Maria Louisa? Of the painting? You know which?"

"Never!"

"Grandmother Rachel, maybe?"

"Never in a million years. Look at the shape of her eyes — "

Whisper from someone. "You can't see her eyes, she's asleep!"

"I think she looks like Dona Emilia. Girls usually look like their mothers, don't they?"

"Of course this scraggly hair will fall out, it always does."

"It's not scraggly!" — hissingly — "You, Francesca, you can say the silliest things, how can you come out with such words?"

"Hush. Hush. You'll wake Baby."

"And I think Baby looks just like Papa! See her determined chin? Just like mine! The way you talk I might have had nothing to do with it."

"Dona Emilia, let me kiss your hands, what a perfect mother you shall be. Just like this perfect creature here."

"And when did you start addressing me as Dona Emilia, Paolo? When was that? And why? You, a friend of the family, the oldest I know! My beloved Paolo, it feels good to call you *Uncle*."

"More beloved than I, your rightful husband?"

"Oh, now you're being silly, José Manuel! Don't listen to him, Paolo."

"You are kind ... too kind ... Emilia."

"No. I'm not and you know it! You old naughty!" — still playfully —"You shall be Baby's godfather." She elbowed him rakishly.

"Baby might need somebody as *raffiné* as you Paolo. And you know who is going to be her godmother? Guess! I bet you'll like the choice, you old rascal! Give up? It will be my very best sister, Dominica, Mother Superior." With a smile, "Yes. Yes. It's true! I spoke to her. She's accepted."

"If you have to talk so much, get out of here, you'll wake Baby."

"We're leaving. We're going right away."

"Let me kiss your hands again. What wisdom! You grew up quickly, it must be motherhood. But jokes aside, I'm honored — deeply honored."

- Voices fade away -

Old cousin, Ana Maria Isabella, stayed with the bassinet. The wrinkled hand, ringless, pushed gently back and forth. Fine, batiste flounces waved with the movement of air. Delicate masses of old Valancienne lace tickled Baby's chin. Honeyed smell of late autumn roses came from the garden beyond the open windows.

Soon after, Baby was christened Maria Beàtricé Dominica. Around her the family, in a tight ring. Later, they partook of the meal served on heirloom china.

"Wasn't the ceremony beautiful? I'm ashamed to say I cried." From old cousin Ana Maria Isabella.

"I didn't think there were still enough dishes to go around. Each time the set comes out of hiding a plate or two disintegrates."

"Francesca, you'll never change. Whenever you open your mouth something unpleasant slips out."

"And you, Maria Leonora, you are a flatterer. You want to please. You'll never admit that our family's money is gone. Gone. Gone. Why else would you live so far away from Lisbon? You flatterer."

From Uncle Carlos, "Hush, hush ladies, you mustn't fight." Turning to his left, "You are right, Ana Maria Isabella. The ceremony was very touching."

Paolo wafted the wine goblet under his powerful nose. Inhaled deeply. Consummate connoisseur. Said nothing.

II

Within a few weeks José Manuel gave his wife the company car for the day. She was the only one of the family's women who knew how to drive. Dona Emilia went to the villa in Estoril to fetch the crib. Cousin Ana Maria Isabella tagged along.

"You'll never find it. I know exactly where it's put away, I covered it up myself. And I should have a look-see around the house. Poor house, how it suffers. Empty rooms. Roof leaks when it rains. Old Cristobal runs around with pots and pans to catch the water. I mentioned it to Uncle Carlos, but you know him. At his age, he wants his peace — can't bear to talk about selling it either. And the garden is gone to seed. We really should sell it."

"You're so sweet, dear Ana Maria Isabella. You worry about things. Pray for a rich American to fall in love with the old relic. Let him beg us to sell. I could use some money, so could everybody. Better start praying."

After dusting and waxing the beautiful bed regained its rosewood patina. Christening robe, laces and batiste flounces from the bassinet washed by caring and knowledgeable hands. Rolled in dark blue tissue. Put away for the next infant of the family.

Paolo came dutifully for visits. Tickled Maria Beàtricé under the chin. Made noises demanded from a godfather. When Baby took hold of his finger in her little hand and smiled into Paolo's face his attitude changed. He became seriously interested. His strong, well-kept hand delicately massaged the little girl's tummy. Whispered into the sweet-smelling neck. "Soon I'll take you to the opera. We'll sit in the best box. Do your growing up, I'll do the rest." His visits, more frequent. Until every day he was with the child at least an hour. As soon as she saw his face Maria Beàtricé demanded to be picked up. Eagerly stretching little arms. Kicking pink feet.

He called it his bewitching hour. When Baby relaxed after bath, fragrant with soap and body powder, pink, pliant, felt cloud-light in his arms. Expecting and getting his full attention. Godfather and godchild alone. First he kissed her every single finger and every little toe. Then he suckled every little finger and every single toe. Caressed silky-fine skin. "Grow up little girl. Grow up. Paolo is going to show you a beautiful world. We shall watch the ballet. We shall eat pink ices. We shall listen to music. We shall eat cream pastry."

Cousin Ana Maria Isabella shook her grizzled head.

"I never saw a godfather give so much time to a child."

"Paolo is generous with his time," came from Dona Emilia. "As a mother I approve. My child, my wonderful child, deserves the best, whatever Paolo can give her. Did you ever eavesdrop on them? I'm not ashamed, I did. Do you know he talks to Baby about music? I wish her father gave her half as much attention. But no, José Manuel has time, but only for his American bosses." Francesca added, "Those two are besotted with each other. Did you notice the tantrum she threw when he did not show up on time?"

For her second birthday Paolo took a beautifully dressed little girl to a ballet matinée. They sat in a box. Maria Beàtricé, bewildered. So many people. Plush seats. So many bright lights. So much gilt. A flowing stream of unknown people. Confused, she squirmed and wiggled in her seat. Straining her neck to see better. Paolo whispered, "Little one, would you see more sitting on my lap?"

"Yes Paolo. That's much better."

From then on, the child was taken to other matinées. Opera. Concerts. Always boldly slipping off her seat and into Paolo's lap. Wriggling herself into a most comfortable position. Smilingly looking up sideways into his face. Obviously flirting, as little ones are wont to do. Searching for confirmation of total well being. After the performance it became a custom to wander into the Ritz's Tea Room. For refreshments. Waiter guiding them to the same, small, round table she pointed out with her little finger. Near the window.

The ladies of the family in and out of each other's houses. Visiting. Gossiping. Playing canasta. The little one giving advice, getting the hang of the game. Her hand not big enough to hold a fan of cards. "But you just wait. Soon, soon. Such a smart child, she retains anything she hears." The ladies beamed. "And the way she coordinates her clothing. Colors have to match, did you notice?"

Paolo took her to antique shows.

"I used to buy a lot of this stuff, but no more." He smilingly waved off dealers wanting to do business with him. "Maria Beàtricé, put your hand here, under the drawer of this desk. Do you feel how rough it is? How unfinished? And look at it well, not many 17th century pieces float around still."

"What happened to your cane, Paolo? The one with the gold knob? Where is it? You always carried it around."

"It's broken. Had to take it for repairs to old Lawrenco." But nobody ever saw the cane with the gold knob again.

He bought tickets for every performance of quality scheduled for Lisbon in the coming year. And arranged ballet lessons. "I want you to acquire lightness of movement, grace, my beautiful one," he said. She met Markova after a gala performance when Paolo took her backstage. Hugged the autographed photograph to her chest. "I'll cherish it all my life," she said. After dance lessons, Paolo took a sweaty, tired, hungry Maria Beàtricé to his rooms. Crooned to her. First we shall take a bath. See the pretty bath salts I have for you? Wrapped her in a large, fluffy bathrobe. "Now you lie on my bed while I bring your supper. Rest. Rest, my little one." Took her home, practically asleep.

Emilia protested. "She had no supper. She must eat!"

"She did, she did eat, my dear Emilia."

A *Portrait of a Burgher* painted by Cranach vanished from Paolo's wall. "What happened to it? Where is it?" "I had to send it away for cleaning," he said. But it did not come back.

III

It was time to start school. She became a day-boarder at the convent. Her Aunt Domenica, the Mother Superior. Scholastically excellent, she knew how to read and write. She knew librettos of classic operas. Contents of Lisbon's museums. Fascinated with histories of Stuarts, Bourbons, Hapsburgs, never tired of more details. "Tell me more Paolo, tell me more." But her conduct, a calamity. An initiator of every prank, every transgression. Ruled her class of peers who followed her sheepishly. When the other mothers complained Uncle Paolo took everybody for tea to the Ritz and everybody was smiles again. Thinking herself invulnerable, she shrugged her shoulders. What will Auntie do to me? Sat in Domenica's sparse office practically every other day. Willful. Stubborn. But oh so sweetly smiling, so polite. "Yes, Auntie. No, Auntie." Had to be forgiven. Promised again and again never to do it again.

IV

Who is it who understands me? Paolo. He is the only one. Takes me the way I really am. Approves all I do, all I say. Mother, Domenica, all other Aunties criticize me. Do this — do that. Be good. Be a good girl. Why don't they see I don't want to be a goody-goody? It's boring! They all bore me! Only Paolo. With a thrill and a shiver she remembered little games they played. Secret games.

Passing his study one afternoon she noticed the naked wall. "What happened to your Art Deco collection? Why aren't the vases here on the wall?"

"I got tired of them. We'll buy other things. Sometime. Together. In the meantime, painted dark green the color of your eyes, the wall will be a perfect background for your photographs."

Grateful she did not notice the absence of the Aubusson carpet. But she was tired. Eager to rest on his bed. Before their concert. He thought she might never notice.

V

Maria Leonora came for a visit. Looked odd, dowdy, old-fashioned. One could guess immediately she lived in the provinces. And why is she crossing herself at every opportunity? It's silly. Francesca jumped at her.

"Stop this. You make us nervous with this crossing. You cross yourself all the time. Is it your sins you're expiating? Is it ours? We are not sinners. You behave like a peasant. Are you now flattering the Holy Trinity? Soon you'll be on your knees begging for only God knows what. Maria Beàtricé, I want you to remember this as a lesson — do you know what is sinful? Not to enjoy life is sinful! Remember it well! Not to brush your hair properly as you're being taught is sinful. When you're given beautiful hair take good care of it! I hope they don't teach you a lot of nonsense in the convent. Your Aunt Domenica wears her silk lingerie under the Ursuline habit — I know it for a fact. I looked in when she was packing to move away. God is not interested in her underthings." She went on and on.

Emilia entered with a tray full: almond cookies, *crème brûlée*, coffee.

"What did I miss? Francesca, are you giving a lecture again? I heard you as far as the kitchen. Maria Leonora, you look like you're going to cry. Why? What happened? Never mind, have some good strong coffee. Don't mind Francesca."

Emilia thought about it for a while. Something was missing in her life. What? A home run smoothly. Maria Beàtricé fully occupied. José Manuel hardly ever home. Probably chasing a snippet of a girl, like some other men, not realizing how stupid it made him appear. Never mind. Can't be helped. Emilia sighed deeply. As long as philandering was done with discretion. What a crazy world!

The ladies settled around two large tables. To play canasta. When will I tell them? Serving coffee she looked at the familiar faces. It seemed the right moment.

"Listen girls, I have something important to tell you."

From somebody, with a twitter of laughter, "What is it Emilia, are you pregnant?"

"Oh, don't be silly! And please don't interrupt me. Listen. I, Emilia, have decided to work as an interior decorator."

"Oh! Why?"

"Everybody knows me for my good taste. I'll show them what I can do with it. You all can help me. This is serious! Francesca, you too, keep quiet! Boutiques, tavernas, the new condos in Albufeira, I want to decorate them all! Who knows? I might make enough money to buy me a *Deux Chevaux*. That would be fun! Anyway, it's up to you all to tell 'the world' Dona Emilia is in business!"

VI

Maria Beàtricé was eleven years old. She became moody. Started to menstruate. Started to write poetry. Started to paint delicate pastels. Sulking. Up one day. Down the other. Francesca called her "our own Sarah Bernhardt". Acting a teenager. Slinking through rooms with hooded eyes, flinging shoulders, tossing her abundant hair. Full of childish defiance. Definitely growing up. "From now on," she demanded, "call me Beàtricé. Only Beàtricé. No more Maria Beàtricé. That's finished." Almost rude.

Observing her, Paolo seemed to lose his bounce, his youthfulness. Still, when alone, they cuddled, nuzzled, kissed, touched as before. But there was a subtle difference. Noticeable to Emilia. She took him aside one afternoon at a family party. "Don't. Don't be like this!" she said, "I recall when I was her age. Do you remember? Do you really remember?"

His eyes misted over. "Yes, dearest Emilia, I do."

"You, Paolo, were ten years my senior. Suddenly I grew up, did not want to play that way with you anymore. But you were so sweet, so tender." She lightly touched his cheek. "I'll never forget, that's why I chose you for her godfather. Beàtricé will come around. She loves you. You're her mentor, her idol. It's only a phase."

VII

He sold the entire collection of signed Lalique sculptures. Twelve-year-old Beàtricé became the youngest patroness of the newly established Gulbenkian Museum. For a round sum of donated money. Started to read Petrarch. Sonnets. Imagined herself to be his Laura. Became thoughtful. Paolo looking on, subdued. Sad.

One afternoon after her dance class she bounded out of school with a bunch of girls. Saw Paolo. Waiting for her as always.

"Is that your Uncle, Beàtricé?"

"Uncle? Nooo! That's my godfather!"

And she called out to him: "I'm going with the others to the ice cream parlor. Jocko's American. Bye-bye." And gaily waved herself off. He tried to be nonchalant but it did not work. Time was gaining on him.

VIII

It had to happen. Soon after, it did happen. If it had not been for the short sharp pain ... so that's what sex means? Is that what we girls were talking about in whispers? So that's **IT**? Felt quite proud of herself. So it's over and done with? Oh, how wonderful it is, what bliss, what perfect bliss. She knew what that was as well. It's orgasm — falling — falling — falling — falling into — into heaven. And she loved Paolo, her Paolo. "Mmmmm," she murmured, "mmmmm, Paolo."

"Did it hurt? Did I hurt you, my beloved? I loved you from the first. The moment your baby eyes looked at me, I loved you all those years. More and more with each passing year. You, my only love. If I hurt you, forgive me, but I had to do it. How could I have left you, my Galatea, to a callous, pimply youngster grappling you only for his own pleasure, who would never appreciate you or cherish you as I do? You are my soul, my life, my love."

It felt so good, so warm, so safe in his arms, so lightly held. He caressed her body. Poky shoulder blades under satiny skin. Hips barely marked. Breasts in early bloom.

"If I were one of my Moorish ancestors you would be my bride. Water fountains would be playing in the courtyard. Scented rose petals would be strewn over our bed. Stars would be looking in on us." She giggled. Head half buried in soft pillows.

"Or concubine?" she asked.

"No. Not concubine. My wife."

Under his tutelage the precocious girl, born privileged, became a prodigy. Now she composed poetry in french. Improvised choreography for her dance school. Read voraciously. Growing up. Getting busy. School activities. Parties. Outings. Surrounded by a gang of peers. Bluejeaned. Chattering. Noisy. Watching the professional football team practice on the field. Or eyes following slim-hipped matadors perfecting their skill with the cape. All was fun. Uninhibited. Foolish. Like other girls. Paolo looking on from the sidelines. They were still together at least twice a week but, he asked himself, is this the end? Is it over? And shuddered at the mere thought. Still, when with him, she changed. Pensive. Quiet. Distant. Affecting a romantic pose. Dressed the part. Consciously alluring. Feminine. Is this a game? Because if it is, we are both playing it. She pretends to be grown up. I pretend to be young. He wanted to talk like before. But she, impatient, shrugged her shoulders for an answer. To get her for himself he suggested a picnic. Let's visit your villa in Estoril. She clapped her hands. Like a child. She is toying with me. Knows it hurts — still does it. She acts a woman. She acts a child.

IX

Late one morning he picked her up. She emerged, numerous petticoats swinging, arms full of lacy pillows and a straw basket. A frail vision in white. They drove in silence. He, concentrating on the road. Trembling inside. Like any young lover so near his love would tremble. And she? She threw him brazenly inviting looks. Testing her power. Playing the age-old game. Like poker. Show me your hand.

Under the old pine tree, in the crook of its roots, a white blanket. Between sturdy branches far below, far away the blue eye of the Atlantic. Against rough bark the foamy frill of pillows. She reclined.

Frothy *broderie anglaise* framing her delicate face, neck, hand. Enormous Mediterranean eyes. Above high, rounded forehead dark hair — parted in the middle — brushed out wide like on the head of a Spanish Infanta. The feet of his beloved in pink satin slippers, with droopy, pastel forget-me-nots. She dressed for me, Paolo thought, she wants me to see her this way. Beàtricé ... forget me not ...

Whispered to her, "What are you dreaming about? Is it a gallant knight on a white charger coming to offer you the world?"

She looked into his face. A face she knew so well. A face she loved. The wrinkles around the eyes, along the cheeks. When did he become so old? My dear, poor Paolo, when did it happen?

From then it started. Avoidance. Excuses. Impatience. More excuses. "I have no time Paolo — no time at all."

X

What a row! When the voices in the salon became too loud, Ana Maria Isabella marched in. Straight-backed. Chignon tightly pinned down. Pursed lips disapproving.

"Shush, you two, shush! They can hear you in the street." Firmly closed the two windows. "Emilia, calm yourself, remember who you are! And you, Beàtricé, don't lie. Don't lie to your mother!" and left.

Emilia carried on, not to be interrupted.

"The whole world knows about it. If your best friend, this Mafalda, tells on you, that's the end."

Beàtricé interrupted her. "She is not my best friend. She is not even a friend. I hate her, she is stupid. Follows me around. She doesn't know what she is talking about."

Emilia, taking over. "Are you going to lie to me, Maria Beàtricé Dominica? Lying will make it even worse. Shame on you! Where was your discretion? Great-granddaughter of an Admiral. A family like ours. No woman in our family ever lied. Honor ... heads held high ... *noblesse oblige.*"

Emilia, very incensed, sputtered, "And this, this mother of this, this Mafalda, has the temerity to tell Ana Maria Isabella, to tell ME to keep my daughter at home? It's crazy! What am I supposed to do? Tell Father? If he hears about it! Thank God Uncle Carlos is dead and gone! Do I tell your father? Haven't I enough troubles with him? You don't pay attention to what's happening at home. He's giving the family a lot of worry, seems to like young girls. Oh God! What am I going to do? Should I speak to Paolo?"

Beàtricé in panic. Bursts of loud sobs.

"No, no, mother, please do not tell father. No, no, not Paolo! Please," between loud sobs, "not Paolo!"

Emilia looked at her daughter's face streaming with tears. Felt no pity.

"Never mind those tears. Stop crying. You're not a baby, crying will not help. But explain to me, how could you, so carefully brought up, so fastidious in your taste, how could you? On a bench of the stadium! And with whom? With an old, short, squat football player! How could you! I bet he had bandy legs. They all have! Beàtricé, I look at you and I don't even know you. The shame of it!"

"Mother, please, mother, stop it! Nothing happened. I told you before, nothing, I swear! Nothing happened!"

Emilia, not allowing for interruption, "Why could you not have chosen one of the daFonseca boys? Tell me why not?"

"Mother, I tell you it was ... it was," smothered in hiccups, "it was a whim."

"What? A whim? A whim she tells me! Now I've heard everything!"

XI

The same evening Emilia wrote a long letter. To her friend. The wife of the Commercial Attaché in the Portuguese Consulate. Somewhere in Canada. Now, where is it? Yes, here is the address. It's in Montreal. Just to touch base, so to speak. Let's see what she will come up with. The letter had a veiled appeal to invite her little Maria Beàtricé for a visit. "Don't they plan to have an Expo there? Tell me about it." And so on ... I have to be prepared, thought Emilia.

Beàtricé could not fall asleep. Furious. Heart thumping violently. Went over every word that was spoken. Hers and Emilia's. She does not believe me, my mother. She listens only to herself. She does not listen to me. She made up her mind not to believe me. My own mother. The injustice of it. Not to be believed. I hate her! Mafalda? — inconsequential. Stupid, gossipy Mafalda? She is a nobody. But my own Mother?

Tightfisted with anger and defiance, railed at her mother the only way she could. "I hate her! I hate her!" She is not my mother anymore. Somewhere at the back of her mind, Paolo. Paolo, who cannot be approached. Who can't be spoken to. Subject taboo. Paolo — safe haven. Anchor. Succor. Gone out of her life. The only one who would understand. Sorry for herself, tears in the corners of swollen eyes, she fell asleep.

Next day in school, Beàtricé searched for Mafalda. There she was in a corner. Skulking. With purposeful steps, head held high, she went over. Stood in front of her enemy. Glowering. Tightly compressed lips. Mafalda, not meeting her gaze. Squirming. Beàtricé had to hold back an overwhelming urge to scratch her face, pull her hair, but remembered: *noblesse oblige*! Slowly turned around without a word, heart beating fast, walked away. Proud of herself. Girls whispered. Others snickered. Let them. What do I care? They think I'm done for? That I'm ashamed? Stupid cows. Let them. They do not know me. I'm fine. I'm fifteen years old, almost. School for me? Finished. I know more than the silly teachers. I'm out of here now. Today.

Actually she was not. Not having a plan, not knowing what to do with herself, she attended classes. Spottily. Full days when it pleased her. Half days when bored. Sometimes not at all. Domenica and Emilia conferred. Over the phone. Face to face. How to talk sense to Beàtricé. How to break the barrier? But the girl listened politely without giving any indication of having heard what was said to her. Not answering. Emilia was beside herself. Shaking her daughter's shoulders furiously. "Did you take a vow of silence? Answer me!" There was no way of reaching Beàtricé, no way of punishing her, no way of going back to times before the row.

Domenica, the diplomat. Peacemaker. "Leave her alone, Emilia. I'll speak to the staff. Classes will terminate soon. Till then, let's pretend nothing's happened. She might have trouble with her classmates, but Beàtricé is a clever girl and will find a way with her peers."

And she did. She ignored them. Utterly. Except for Inez. Inez, who sat two seats to her left, slipped a crumpled note into her lap. "I'm with you," it read. "Will you go for a walk with me?" Yes, Inez was her only friend. Sometimes she even skipped school for her sake. Teachers looked the other way, anxious only to reach term's end. At all costs, avoid scandal. Beàtricé. Marked girl. She felt quite well in this role. Dramatic. It suited her to leave school in the middle of the day — saunter over wherever she fancied. Sort of lawless.

If she felt like it she headed towards the stadium of the corrida. To watch the matadors' ballet steps. Dainty shoes practicing. Red cape swishing from side to side. Long muscles of limbs and back taut. Roundness of tight buttocks. She sat holding onto the school books in her lap. Was noticed. So young. So pretty. A schoolgirl. During rest break, this one or that one came over. To have a chat. To joke. Embrace, if allowed. Steal a kiss. Or a feel. She permitted this much, giggled, not more, then abruptly got up and left. Came back the next day. Or not. It seemed the matadors acquired a new kind of fan — a classy girl. But Lisbon being Lisbon, someone noticed, someone told, someone brought the tale home.

XII

Emilia sat in her bedroom alone. With closed eyes. Concentrating.
"I will not panic. I will be as calm as I can. I won't even talk to Beàtricé — useless. This rebellion can't be harnessed, her behavior is unacceptable. Stubborn, bent to her own destruction. She knows the rules. This is Portugal! One has to conform, be discreet. Who does she think she is? Thank God my letter to Montreal brought such a warm response. Thank God it's so far away. Thank God I have friends. By the time she comes back to Lisbon people might have forgotten her misbehavior — but I doubt it — I doubt it."

XIII

Communication between mother and daughter — minimal. For weeks only the most necessary words were spoken. One morning, Beàtricé sat down to breakfast. On the plate before her, under the napkin, an unfamiliar envelope. From the airline. From Trans Air Portugal. Her heart skipped a beat. What does it mean? With narrowed eyes, she looked up at Emilia across the table.
"What is this?"
"Open the envelope, you'll see. Read it."
Eyes scanned the paper. Her name was specified. It was a ticket to Montreal, Canada. Calculating the date.
"But mother, departure is in four days!"
"Yes, it's unfortunate, isn't it? TAP flies only once a week to Montreal. It will have to do."
If looks could burn, Emilia would have turned to a cinder. With tightly compressed lips, Beàtricé jumped up from her seat. Overturned chair crashed to the floor. Door banged shut behind her. Emilia, with a bitter smile, sat alone at the table. Grimly thought, "It's checkmate time, my daughter."

XIV

Her name was called on arrival. To come to TAP's flight counter. She was expected. The Consulate's chauffeur loaded her bags and, politely smiling, locked the door behind her.

"Drive slowly, please, I would like to see where I am. You say this is called Downtown? It's so different from Lisbon. It's so new. Do they have old houses here? Is it still far?"

"No, no, it's very near. You will love it here, Miss, it's a city for young people — very lively. Oh, you see, here. Here we are."

Embraced warmly by Clara. "Let me see you! Just like my darling Emilia. You know, she was my maid of honor. So pretty. We had to keep altering her dress — she was already pregnant with you, Beàtricé. Yes, our friendship goes back a very long time. Let me show you around. This is your room. It has this enormous bathroom, lucky for you. Side entrance from hall. Complete independence as you see. A reception tonight, are you too tired to join us?"

Beàtricé took an immediate liking to Mother's friend, this Clara, so warm, chattery, friendly.

"I'm fine. I'd love to come."

Parties, receptions, more parties. Montreal was jumping. Metro progressing. Expo in the making. Place des Arts so new — all added to the excitement. To a modern tempo. No time to miss sleepy Lisbon. She met a slew of people. Singled out a small *coterie* of homosexuals who readily adopted her.

"Am I lucky! With you guys I can talk. I can talk ballet! Bulgari! Paintings. Good food. Let me cook a real Portuguese dinner for you!"

They reciprocated by inviting her to the theater, concerts. It was quite a sight to observe, this entrance of late comers. Almost when the lights dimmed they trooped in. First down the aisle, Beàtricé, dressed to the nines. Exquisitely made up. Tight turban underlining her fine bone structure. A few steps behind, three or four elegantly tailored men. Dark-suited. Made-to-order shirts. Plain, subdued ties. Perfect background for Beàtricé. Heads turned. People whispered. More so if one of her *entourage* wore a kilt. An outstanding group. Always seated center front. One of the new friends, a doctor, told her of a girl sick with Multiple Sclerosis. Exactly her age. Mother working afternoons. The crippled teen alone for some hours. Beàtricé cried bitter tears. Here am I, so thrilled with life while this poor girl, condemned, suffers. I could be her! Phoned. Katie's mother, overwhelmed with gratitude, took the call.

"Of course," with heartfelt thanks, "what a Godsend you are. Come over, the key will be with the concierge."

It was not far. A walk around the corner. Whenever she could, she dropped in. Sometimes Katie was still in bed. Beàtricé dressed her. Pushing limp feet into warm slippers. Lifted wasted body into a chair.

"Oh, this is better. I didn't feel like getting up today, but now you are here, it's different."

She read to her. Joked. Told tall tales. Painted both their faces as clowns, as Charlie Chaplin. Anything to make Katie laugh!

"Did they tell you the truth about cars? Did they? I bet they did not! Did they tell you that inside, under the hood, there really is no motor? Did they tell you that? No motor at all. There, under the hood is a bunch of chipmunks. Yes, yes, chipmunks. Most of the time the sweet little things sleep cuddled up close. But the moment somebody turns the key and pushes a button, they wake up! Whoa, whoa, quick, quick, they start running! Little feet churning ahead, just like this, just like that, and they make the car go."

Buying a pastry for Katie, she met a young girl behind the counter. "I haven't seen you here before. Did you just start working?"

"It's my father's shop. He is the *pâtisser*. I come in emergencies. So here I am!"

They became friends. Just like Inez, Lucy looked up to her adoringly. I love the way you dress. And your make up! You're so sure of yourself. Sophisticated. I'm born here but we are Ukrainians — sort of old-fashioned at home. Beàtricé thought, what a perfect confidante to have.

"I'm so happy to have met you."

Showered her with gifts. Nothing store-bought. Only, "You like this sweater? Take it. You need this skirt? Take it. I have a similar one." Her life was full. Amusing. She did not think of Portugal. The two met at Café Carmen often. Sometimes after visiting with Katie.

One day, running home, trying to shake off the memory of Katie's deteriorating body, a sudden shower. More than a shower, more like a downpour. And I'm wearing my pretty, Italian sandals — bet the little straps are glued-in. Gee whiz! I can't soak them this way. Here is Carmen, hope Lucy's here. She looked in. No. Lucy was not there. Then I won't sit down. I'll wait here. Anyway, it's late. Looked at her wristwatch. Under the arch in the doorway waiting for the rain to stop. It looked pretty grim. The sidewalk was awash with water. I can't walk in this rain. Too late for Lucy to come. Looking out, no taxi coming and impatient, fidgeted. She felt somebody at her side. Looked up. A tall, youngish man. She'd noticed him before, always sitting in a corner. Reading. Was it a Hungarian magazine? Over a Cappuccino. Familiar. He smiled at her.

"It's wet, isn't it? If you want me to give you a lift my car is right here. In the lane. Have to go home myself."

"Oh, I could not put you out of your way."

"You wouldn't. Once I'm in the car, a few more minutes doesn't make a difference." After a pause, he added, "You often come to Carmen."

"Yes, I do. It's European. It's like home."

"I've noticed you. Here is my apartment house," stopping the car, "I wonder if you mind waiting a few minutes? Have to make a telephone call. Or better still, why don't you come up for a few minutes? Might be more amusing than sitting in the car."

"Yes, why not." said Beàtricé and followed him to the elevator. Opening his apartment door he let her in first. Like a well brought-up man should. Then stepped in behind her. And before she could realize what was happening he turned the key, locking the door. Slipped it out of the lock and into his coat pocket. Mouth half-open in utter amazement she realized, in a flash, she'd become his prisoner. Furious. Mad. With both hands, pushed him against the wall. Hard. And shouted, "Are you crazy? Let me out! This instant! Open the door!" His smile became a leer. His teeth showed. Like dog teeth. He lunged after her. She darted away. Around the table. Running. Tripping. Almost falling. Handbag dangling from shoulder strap, flying. Disbelief. It's happening to me. This is for real. If he catches me I'll kill him. I'll gouge his eyes out. I'll kill him. And she fell. She was done for. She fought. She kicked. He pinned her arms down. This is the end. She closed her eyes not to see his hideous, ugly face above her. I'm like a butterfly pinned alive under glass. God, let me die ... I want to die ... The key. How can I get the key? She couldn't. His jacket was abandoned on the carpet. Out of reach. "Mother of God, let him finish..."

When he was done she managed a smile, fervently praying, the door — the door — open the door.

"You liked it?"

"I loved it." she answered through clenched teeth. "But now I must go."

She flew out of the building. Not knowing how, she made it. Here she was. Her own room. Her own bathroom. Here she collapsed.

Huddled on the floor beside the bathtub — sobbing. Hand fumbled with faucets. Steaming hot water filled the tub. Half dressed, half stripped. Submerged. Choking. Submerged again. With a sponge. Then with a bath brush she scrubbed her body. Between her thighs, she scoured the flesh raw. Wanted to flay it. Bruised mouth offending, she tore at it blindly. Till blood showed red on the brush. Between sobs, moans, between weepings, she heard herself calling, "Paolo, Paolo, Paolo."

EMILY

Will you have something more to eat? No? I'm also full. Just some more coffee, please.

I like this drugstore. Don't you? It's homey.

So. you're asking what's the purpose in telling this story? And why now?

The answer is simple. Because almost half a century has passed. Because life is different. Because I knew the people involved. Because I played a role. Finally, because the tale wants to be told.

I see you smile. Never mind. It's all right — if you see it that way — yes — to amuse you.

Where was I?

Ah, yes, the car. Do you remember a little car called Minx? Not even vaguely? How silly of me. Of course not! You are too young for that. See, the car and the story were both of the fifties. Anyway, to come back to the red car which gave my friend freedom, it was a busy woman's car. At that time ladies wore hats, gloves, went to luncheons, sat on committees. Did valuable charity work. Fashion shows — the favorite, auctions, concerts. All brought money needed for a cause.

Permit me to generalize. They usually had two children. Employed two "live-ins" at home. Life ran smoothly. Thursday afternoons and Sundays till midnight, were help's time out. Free.

Good wives. Conscientious housekeepers. Good mothers. Husbands, generous providers. Showing unfailing loyalty to their women. Hanky-panky invisible. To make waves — taboo. The "gals" as they referred to themselves, had cupboards full of "outfits". Each for a designated purpose. Wore more *maquillage* than needed. When daring, applied turquoise to upper eyelids. And so did gorgeous Emily. And gorgeous she was.

Yes! Yes! Emily is the heroine of my story! She is my friend with the red Minx!

She was tall. Stately. Small head sporting a slinky, short haircut. Unusual. Like a boy's. Long, ruby-red fingernails flashing. Green eyes mocking. Behind a veil of cigarette smoke. Voice husky. Alluring. Too busy for nonsense. Dashing around. Doing things.

What? What nonsense, you are asking?

Well, silly girl! — flirting. That nonsense! She had no time for flirting. Yes. I thought so. A lost art. Avidly practiced in Europe. If you would only know how much spice it adds to life ... still ... but coming back to Emily.

Yes, the entertaining. There was a lot of that. Mostly cocktail parties. And imagine, real cocktails were served! Not like now. What are we drinking now? White wine. White wine only. Sort of bloodless, don't you think? Anemic. At the time they drank Manhattans, Martinis, Stingers, Whisky-Sours, Rum & Cokes ...

Laugh all you want — it seems funny to me, too. So why not laugh? Anyway, that's how it was.

At parties men congregated with men. Women grouped with women. Marginal intermingling of sexes. At any rate, not visible.

Friday after dinner "dirty" movies shown. At home. Among close friends. Awful stuff. Sort of *samisdat*.

Do you really want to know about live eels and other nastiness? I don't think you need to learn about that lot. Let's go back to the story.

Saturday night everybody met everybody. At Ruby Foo's. Or dancing at the Normandie, atop the Mount Royal Hotel. Very New Yorkish.

Sunday, dedicated to *The New York Times*. Paper strewn all over wall-to-wall living room carpet. Mixed abundantly with children's toys. A proper day of leisure. (Maid's day out, remember?) Emily doing like others. As was the fashion. She, with quick intelligence, with so called "smarts," organized, orderly. Whose calendar-journal was picture perfect. Who, with minimal effort showed best results within the group, in whatever she undertook. She, who never, to my knowledge, was ever muddled. Or lost for words. She, also, had two children. A school-age boy, Eddie, and a little doll-like girl, Annette.

I remember when her son needed school uniforms. She ordered a taxi to pick him up after school. Met the child in front of outfitter's shop on St. Catherine Street. Later, sent him back same way to the maid waiting at the house door. One has to appreciate how she controlled situations. Freeing her for other commitments.

Yeah ... yeah ... I agree. And I have to admit, you're right. She had to have, and she did have, a down-side. Don't we all? I loved her.

But not everybody did. I'm going to describe her with a critical eye. The lady was too visible. That's it! I said it!

No, dear girl, don't call me charitable. I'm not. This was my friend. For sake of truth I have to admit Emily was a bit brassy. A bit overdone. And those are words as plain as I can muster. But you be truthful as well. Wouldn't you be, if placed in Emily's shoes? Particularly if you would have known how her husband adored her. He simply worshipped her. It's often said about husbands. In his case it was true. Emily was Alpha and Omega of Ralph's life. Which makes a woman — here you have to rely on an older woman's experience — and I'm old enough — a woman loved like she was loved, becomes self-assured. Bold. Strong. To be loved. Given this kind of support one is armed against any and all vicissitudes of life.

I can see from your face — you disapprove. All right — if you wish — take it for a lecture. But look around. How is it now with your sisterhood? It should have changed. Did it?

A while back I mentioned Emily's name to one of her contemporaries. Sure, a woman! Do you know how she described my friend? "... this detestable person with deep cleavage and red talons ... this husband stealer! ..."

Now! Truly! That woman was plain envious. Catty. I, I of all people would have known about husband stealing. Remember? — I was Em's best friend. Her only true friend.

You're doubting how I could have known that?

Easy. All those ladies surrounding each other at meetings, at parties. Talking daily on the phone. Children's birthdays, dresses, recipes and so on. No time to develop real relationships. What you would call sisterhoods. Potential threat and rivalry came from all sides. There was no safety. A careless word blurted out could mean a social disaster.

Gossip? Don't even ask. Gossip was rampant. (As long as one could not put a finger on it ... or point a finger ...) No. Friendship was then as it still is, a rare flower. To be cultivated. Kept separate. Close to one's chest. For special heartaches — a special person. I'm not saying I was this special person — no — but I did have one point qualifying me above others — I did not belong. I was not a member of "the group". Knew most of them. True. But only superficially. I was an outsider. A working woman. Secrets and confidentialities stopped with me. Nowhere else to go. Safe.

Yes, please, I'll have some more coffee. Thank you. It's nice to lunch where you're known. Don't you think? Just remind me to leave a double tip. The girl deserves it. Will you have some pie? No? Yes, the everlasting weight problem. Mine too. So where was I?

Yes. The fatal day. Yes. There always is something to set off a chain of events. In this case it was a hat. Emily picked up her new spring hat. Divine. It was simply divine. Actually, didn't make up her mind to go, but once she put on this wispy, cloud-white concoction of silk violets, once she saw how flatteringly it framed her face, she decided. What the heck! It's too beautiful not to give it a proper airing! I'll go! Quickly ran her Minx home. Changed dress. Repaired face. Kissed the children getting ready for early supper and off she went.

Was late. Very late. The large rooms chock-full of people. At a glance, noticed faces daily encountered. Some she had not seen in donkeys' years. A sprinkling of new heads. Hello here. A kiss. Hello there. A hug. Slowly she ploughed away towards her hostess. Betty leaning against the Baby Grand.

Hey! Wait a minute! There was an interesting man next to her. "Who is the fellow talking to Betty?" she asked the nearest standing.

"Emily, don't tell me you don't know him!"

Yes, of course! She knew the name. Knew who he was. So well known. Actually famous. A research physician. So that's how he looks? Not bad at all. Very presentable. And here he was and she stood in front of him. Her friend, Betty, barely reaching his chest. His head turned down towards her. Talking. Then he lifted his face. Looked straight at Emily. Emily looked back at him. No soft planes in that face. Kind brown eyes. Wide, generous mouth. A man for all seasons, came to Emily's mind.

Believe me, dear girl, that's what she told me! "A man for all seasons." Those were her very own words.

I agree with you. Quite an odd saying. Shakespearean, strange. Not fitting a cocktail party. But there you are ... So, he looked at Emily. Met her slightly bewildered gaze. His brown eyes were more than just kind. They were penetrating. Seeing right into her. Unsettling. Disturbing. Both remained like this. Eyes locked. Emily felt her face get hot. Heart racing. She could not look away. That's when the thunderbolt struck. She knew it. It's him! She felt it in her gut. That's THE MAN. God, that's MY MAN. He took her proffered hand in his. Large hand. Warm. Strong. Her own felt like a homing pigeon. It felt good in his. Like it belonged there. It did not want to let go. And so they held on to each other ... When Betty turned away, talking to somebody on her right, he said, "I want to see you. Please. Alone.

Would you? Would you phone my office? Tell the secretary I asked you to phone..."

There was no time for more. Still they stood facing each other. But talking? No, talking was impossible.

Next day, you guessed it, my dear. She came racing here to tell me. All. The whole story. Flashed. Not very coherent. "I did not sleep one whole night," she said.

"Em, what's happening to you? What's going on? You sound strange. Not like your own self."

And strange was a lukewarm word to describe my Em. We sat here. At this very same table. Lucky, I'm working around the corner. I could always run over here. At a moment's notice. To be her sounding board. Because, you see, at this point, believe me, she did not know what struck her. This situation was utterly unfamiliar. She needed to hear her own feelings turn into words, bounce off a solid wall. I presented that wall.

Of course she wouldn't listen to reason, to my warnings.

"It's madness, Em. It's dangerous," I told her. "You have a family. He's got a wife, and I hear, three children. You both can destroy your lives."

To no avail. She looked past me. Into the air. Tomorrow. Tomorrow they'll meet. She mentioned a small side street hotel. So that's how it started. So that's how it went.

Please don't be judgmental. Whatever it was, it was not a "sordid affair," as you put it. As a writer you owe it to yourself to look beyond the obvious. For a different approach. Easy to say "a sordid affair". To make it commonplace. It was not. It was love. Desperate because of circumstances. But love it was. You say devious? Yes. You're right. I have to admit. They both had to be devious.

Days passed. Emily did not come or phone. I knew what it meant. Heaven. Euphoria.

A question bothered me. How long? How long can it last? As a writer and a woman, you understand, this was not a set-up for life. Don't get me wrong, I knew they were in love — how does it go? Love with a capital "L"? To me there was a "but" with a capital "B" as well.

Time flew. Then one day she came. Superficial calm belied her dancing eyes. Her beatific smile. "Let's have coffee," she said. Just looking at her told me it's going to mean 2-3 hours in the drugstore. Told my secretary to fetch me if needed. They knew where.

I told you before — this table became our table. We sat. I looked at her. Emily was radiant. With closed eyes, hugging her shoulders, she swayed in the seat across from me. Trying to paint her bliss with words. Describing how they clung to each other. How they talked and talked and could not tear themselves away from each other. Only two hours. At best two hours. That's the time they had for each other. She, leaving her Minx around the corner, as far as possible. He, grabbing a taxi.

Hm, you know? It's funny how often I mention Em's car. I realize this very moment why I do it. I myself had a car. Even smaller. A little bug. Way back. Home. My Simca.

There you are ...

Anyway, while I was listening to Emily's story, coffee grew cold in front of her. She sat, clinging to her shoulders with both arms. Like those arms would be his arms. Like she would be holding on to the imprint of his embrace. Not letting go.

I asked about home. Her children? Her good Ralph? She knew I liked her husband. Such a nice man ... yes, she knew. She assured me:

"All's well. He has no reason to suspect anything. I feel a great tenderness towards him. "I'm being kinder now than before. Protective. You are so right. Such a nice man ... . My children? I'm not robbing them of my presence. Hugs, kisses, my time, story readings — just as before. Like always."

But on her the strain showed. She lost weight.

"When I'm asked, I tell them, 'it's a special diet.' " And she smiled. Her face smiled. Eyes looking somewhere beyond.

There was nothing for me to say. I just listened. Except for a small warning ... "watch out — be careful," I murmured.

The dramatic, cryptic telephone call came in the evening. Her voice strained. Muted. "Wait for me. I'll come as soon as Ralph leaves for the office."

Something awful must have happened. Obviously she could not speak. Ralph was probably in the next room.

A few minutes past nine she showed up. Looked terrible. No make-up. At this early hour there was no chance she might encounter any of her acquaintances. At least let's thank God for some anonymity. And some mercies.

"What's happened," I asked. "What's going on? You look very tired. You sound even worse ..."

"I didn't sleep," she said. "You don't know what happened ..." she paused ... "Yesterday. We both left the hotel at the same time. You might think we could get together often? You're wrong. At the most twice a week. That's how often. So don't be surprised we could not separate just like one-two-three. We were careless. We held hands. We looked at each other, face to face. We kissed. This at the entrance of the hotel. Don't look at me this way," she said .... "We did. We kissed. And the unthinkable happened. A business friend of Ralph's, just imagine! Across the street, at this very moment, left the watchmaker's shop. Can you beat it? There are so many moments in a day. Oh, God, why did it have to be exactly this moment? On the other side of the street? And he saw us! You know what he did? This 'friend?' He promptly drove to Ralph's office and told him. Out of the goodness of his heart. A friendly act of information .... He told him what he saw — what it meant. Ralph got mad. Plain, crazy mad. Wanted to kill him. To punch his face in. Shook him by the shoulders. Shouted, 'You liar! You liar! How dare you! I'll kill you! Don't you ever come near me! I'll kill you! All lies, lies, lies!' And threw him bodily out.

"Ashen- faced, shaking, he came home. Upstairs, I was reading to the children. I was at the first fairy tale. 'What are you doing home so early?' and I looked up at him. Saw the storm in his face. I tell you, he was trembling. I felt doomed. At the moment I felt — no! I knew. This is the end. I managed to say, 'What happened?' That's all I could manage ...

"Ralph shoved the children out. To the landing. Called down to the maid, 'Take the kids.' And very carefully, deliberately, slowly, closed the door. We were alone. Only then did he tell me. I thought I'd die. There was a searing pain in my chest. I wanted to die. Ralph's voice was very low. Threatening. Shivering with rage and I don't know what else, he asked me point blank if it was true. He looked right into my eyes. I know Ralph. I could read him. He was devastated. Poor Ralph ... I knew he wanted me to deny it. He wanted me to erase the story he just heard. He wanted me to erase his pain. I felt so weak I thought my life blood must be draining away. Looked down at the floor. At my feet. Expecting to see a pool of blood. There was no blood. I had to face my husband's eyes. And I knew I had to rescue him. I had to rescue me. Maybe I could? Could I? I had to try. If? Then I had to deny it. So — so — I admitted it. 'Yes! It was me! Of course it was me. What nerve! This man. Such an idiot. So what? The doctor just left the hotel. Answered a call from some out-of-town patient. So we said, "Hallo". So we shook hands — I had just parked the car — had to go to the watchmaker — remember the old watch? — needs cleaning — I took it in — promised to donate it for the next auction

— what nerve! To assume! — stupid fool! — suspicious idiot! I hate this sort of person!' And the more indignant I became, the more I made sense. I became alive again. Everything depended on my words. My actions. Even on the tone of my voice. Both hands with spread fingers gesturing in the air to underline the imbecility of the denouncer. I was offended. 'It's not what he thought he saw!' I said, in turn becoming mad, 'How dare he? the moron!' Visibly agitated I denied and denied till I saw a spark of relief in Ralph's eyes. He wanted to believe me. And he did believe me."

Emily sat. Spent. Exhausted. Rubbed her forehead in confusion. "But I? Where am I? What am I going to do? How will I live? Who can help me? God in heaven ..." and tears rolled down her face. Fingers of one hand clutching the other. Clenching. Unclenching.

Would you venture to guess what happened later? As a sequence to this fateful day? You guessed it. Bravo! Clever girl. I knew you would. Yes, the nasty part to the story. Rumors. Unsubstantiated. Underhanded. Nothing to "put a finger on" — still ... suspicions ... gossip ...

It went on something like this:

"I've heard about a mystery man. Did you? Do you know anything about that? — Who told you? — Didn't you hear? — She's hiding something — How could she? — I see her practically every other day, she couldn't. Is there really somebody? — Who? — Who is it? — You know what they say? Where there is smoke ... She lost weight, but said it's a new diet. She acts normal — No, she does not! — I've been told it's Ralph's friend — Who is? — The mystery man? — I don't believe it! — Is HE the man? — Who? — Nonsense, the man who said it, he is Ralph's friend, he is not the mystery man — Who is he? Who is this "friend"? I'd love to ask him one or two questions ...."

And on and on. Can you imagine how "the group" buzzed if I, outside it's periphery, heard this much! Still, at every party, concert, gathering, there they were. Ralph and Emily. Together. Acting normal. An aura hovering about them. Keeping "the group" at arms' length. Almost daring them for more than the usual, "Howareyou hellogoodbye." Nobody did. But pressure of prying eyes followed their every move. Do you think two people can play-act under constant scrutiny of their peers? Day in and day out. Did they play-act? How do you know? How did anybody know? Only I. I knew.

Days passed. Unpleasant days. And then, the strained voice of Emily over the phone. By the way, did I ever, while telling you this story, mention the name of Emily's lover? I hope not! I'm going to be very careful about this secret. Some of the participants are still around. It wouldn't do to embarrass anybody, so, my dear girl, *nomina sunt odiosa*. You think you know his occupation? Don't bet on it, my dear. I'm camouflaging this as well. But "doctor" it is — "doctor" he is going to stay. As such, his fame spread. In the United States and well beyond its borders.

As far as Brazil.

Back to my story. When I heard Emily's strained voice again over the phone. "May I come?" Yes. She came. More often. For short spurts. Strange visits. She, sometimes excited with feverish eyes, sometimes depressed, hardly communicative. "I just wanted to see you ..." she said. "I'll tell you later ... I'll tell you tomorrow ..." And so it went. She needed me to hold her hand, that's all. I understood how difficult it was for them to meet. Not like before. Not for two hours. Not any more. How did they meet? I don't know. Presumably just for some minutes. Here. There. Just to keep in touch, to discuss their plight. That's me guessing ...

Till one day Emily floored me again. News. A plan. There was a plan. Apparently the doctor received an invitation from a South American University. A while back. Before he even met Emily. This handsome offer languished in his files. Without comment or reply. Why should he want to leave his city? Career, home, friends, contacts? Take children out of school and plunge into a different culture with a different language? Nonsense. He did not need such a monumental upset. More money? He did not need more. If the change would have spelled relief from his marital difficulties, if it would obliterate years of coldness, of complete lack of communication between him and his wife, yes. Maybe that would have been an inducement. But otherwise it would have meant to take with him the same heavy baggage. The barely existing marital ties strained even more. Not a bargain. No sense to it. But now with dogs barking at their heels. Now with Emily next to him. Now it was a worthwhile plunge. To get away from the untenable situation. From the present. Money counted. Research facilities, new opportunities, immediate deanship, all counted. But mostly, leaving the city counted. To be together, a bonus of unmeasurable proportion.

The offer was accepted with apologies for delay. Papers dispatched for signatures. And Emily was broken up ... voice down to a whisper, she described how he held her hands. Supportive. Strong. Saying:

"It's the only future we have. If we have a future. That's it. Ralph will let you have the children. If not, well, you'll visit here, visit often, you will not lose your kids."

Her fingers squeezed in his palms. All strength of his body seemed to pour into her. But she was incredulous.

"Visit my children?" "My babies??" and collapsed in his arms. Cried inconsolably.

Repeated, "To visit my own children??"

He said, "We have to be strong. There is no other way."

To me she whispered, "I can't give them up — I can't give HIM up — I'll have to go — How can I go? ..."

No, she did not cry. It's strange, she cried with him. Didn't with me when telling the story. She trembled. I slid from my chair to this bench and I held her. One arm clutching her waist in a strong embrace. I held her.

"Listen, listen Emily! Listen carefully. I have to tell you what I think. All this past time you made me a partner of sorts by confiding in me. O.K. I warned you sometimes but did not give advice. Now I have to. Look at me. Pull yourself together. You must think. You can't go! You do not go! If you leave, the law will be against you. Look at me! Listen, you'll lose your children, home and a trusted friend, your Ralph. Don't fool yourself. Ralph will never give you up as well as his kids. Forget it! And when that happens where will your love-passion be after a short while? Imagine! Unknown country, strange culture, language, lifestyle, people, all new, and you alone. He'll have his work. Go to the university, to his lab. He'll have his science, colleagues — but you? You'll only have time. Time for regrets and tears. Where will love and ardor be? Gone. Gone from you. Gone from him. Bridges burned. No going back. Think! Think carefully. You can't go."

Do you think I was cruel? I don't believe so. Remember, it's Emily who came to me. By confessing, asked for what? For complicity? For advice? It was my duty, duty of a best friend to tell her the truth. To save her. She seemed unable to imagine her future life beyond the immediate. She was blinded.

You're right. Common sense pitched against passionate love. Now it sounds fuddy-duddy. Then, it must have been worse. But there you are. I was her friend.

But to no avail.

They went ahead. Secret preparations were made. Final decisions. How much to leave. How little to take. Days folded into each other. The doctor was called away to New York, she told me, "for a few days," and was not happy about it. It was a question of a prestigious international meeting, during which he was delivering a key paper. If it had been longer Emily would have found ways to follow him, but the conference lasted an unspecified "few days". That's what made her unsettled, anxious.

"Oh, forget it — he will be back sooner than you think," I consoled her. "Think of the honour, to read his work before 400 luminaries from around the world. Aren't you proud?"

"Of course, I'm proud, but ..."

I guess she needed his presence in the city.

He left. The New York affair was mentioned on radio and in newspapers — an honor to Canada, etc ... etc...

Next day at noon the radio announcer interrupted the news program:

"We have to interrupt our newscast. Our local doctor, the main speaker at the world conference in New York, collapsed on the podium. Stricken while delivering the introduction to his paper ... massive coronary occlusion suspected ... taken to hospital ... situation grave ... other bulletins on his state of health expected soon ... shall be announced on this program ... stay tuned ... this station will keep listeners informed ... as soon as ..."

Within minutes Emily was at my door. Face drenched in tears.

"I'm going to New York. To be with him. Airport. Come with me to the airport. Have to go. Airport ... " Voice, a hoarse whisper. She turned to go. I, right behind her, following. Didn't have a chance to say a word. Her Minx parked crooked at the curb. Door ajar. I slid in beside her. She, gripping the steering wheel with white knuckled hands. The gears grinding in protest. Started off towards home. Mumbling between tear-choked sobs, "Passport, have to take my passport, only handbag, right away ... I need to ... I have to ..."

"Emily, please, stop for a minute. Stop. Listen to me." Both my hands clutching the steering wheel. Car careening in wide zigzags. On and off the sidewalk. Her face puffed red from weeping, eyes practically closed shut, she didn't see to drive.

"Stop!" I shouted. "Stop this minute, you'll kill us both. You'll be arrested." Both my feet "braking" the car's floor, holding fast to the steering wheel with both hands, I screamed, "You're crazy. You're mad!"

She stopped.

"Listen. Look at me," and I turned her face towards mine.

"Look at me and listen carefully. Y o u c a n n o t g o. Impossible! You can't. Don't you understand what's happening over there? Now, first of all, let's go home. Right now. Let's turn on the radio. Let's hear what's going on in New York."

"But I have to be with him. I have to do something right now. I'll die if I don't do something right away! I can't go on like this! I can't just wait I can't!"

"Emily, listen, wake up. He's got a wife and kids. By now for sure they're flying to join him. You have no place at his side. You can't go. Drive on, we'll listen to the bulletins at home, we don't know what's happening."

"He wants me. I know it. I feel it. He's calling me. Have to do something — my love — my love ..."

"Em, yes, you're right. Let's do something. How much money do you have in your purse? Okay, never mind, all of it! All, as much as there is. You shall buy flowers! Spend all of it! Send them right away to the hospital. Come, drive on. There is a flower shop, corner Sherbrooke and Guy, nobody knows you there. Right here — see it? That's it with the HERMES sticker on the window. Let's go in.

"A note? No. There will be no note. Emily? Are you crazy again?" I brushed away the little card.

"Do you think he will read a note? What's with you? But if he sees all those flowers he'll know they're from you. Who else? For sure he'll know. It's like you being at his side. He'll know. Now, let's go home and listen to the news ..."

We ran into the living room to click the radio open. The announcer's voice in mid-sentence: "... a great loss to the scientific community ... a great loss to Canada ... our sincere condolences ..."

I turned it off.

Emily, with a puzzled look, staring at the box. Standing in the middle of the room and staring. "I didn't say good-bye — I didn't say good-bye," she said. Slowly her face crumpled like a child's. Tears started to flow. Guided to a sofa, she slumped with hunched shoulders. Quietly, weeping uncontrollably. Like a doll with a spent mechanism ... allowed me to lift her legs, to push her entire body into a lie-down position. Covered with a warm shawl. I left her.

You're asking where was Ralph? You guessed it. He drove up. Right then and there.

"Oh, Ralph, dear Ralph! Emily has such a headache. She can hardly see. A bad migraine. I gave her a cold compress. She's lying down. You know how good a doctor I am? — Yes, I am, I'll take care of her. You can go back to your office. I'll phone you later. Or, would you like some

lunch? I'm sure the girls in the kitchen can whip up a sandwich for you... Okay, if you're not hungry, I'll call the office later. Right."
And he left.

Thank God he left. But I knew Ralph. I could read his face. Deep worry was written in that face. Did he know? Yes. Was he apprehensive? Again yes. But, there was nothing he could do, was there?

What followed were telephone calls. The phone didn't stop ringing. I asked myself over and over how is it possible for people, for so called "friends" to be so vicious. As fate would have it, would you believe it? — on this very afternoon, of this fateful day, Betty — remember Betty? Betty had a large party. Like the one in early spring, months ago when Emily decided to air her new spring hat? Remember? Now, at the end of the season, same kind of a party ... She phoned! "Is Emily coming?" All the gals I was acquainted with — all phoned. "Is Emily home? Is she going to Betty's party? Can I pick her up?"

"Oh, yes. Oh, sure. I replayed. Sure she is coming. Unfortunately, she's down with a summer cold — it's going around, don't you know? But yes, she'll be there, with bells on. No, Ralph will pick her up coming from the office. Yes, all puffed up from the cold, but as beautiful as ever, she'll be there ..."

In the kitchen I brewed some tea. Poured the liquid down the drain. Saved the tea-bags in the fridge. To cool off. These, when cold, applied to her swollen eyelids. In the darkened room she rested. With tea-bags on her eyes.

Before I called Ralph at his office to come and fetch Emily, I chose for her the biggest, the flashiest earrings. For the party. For defiance.

She went to the party. Everybody suspected. Nobody knew for sure. And that's it! That's the story! And look at the time, it's ages! We've been here more than two hours. But here it is. The story is finished. Can you do "things" to it? As a writer, I mean ... could you write it?

Yes, phone me. Yes, by all means phone. I took up so much of your time ... but now, run along. It's late. I'll leave the waitress a good tip. Go.

No! Wait! One more word. If you don't phone, I'll understand. You don't like Emily. I can see it. Not many did. Poor Em. Could she choose how she loved? ...

RUTH AND FLORA

A crowd spilled out of the German train. Tripping on rails, ties, pebbled stones, sparse grass of no-man's land. Suitcase in one hand, warm coat on the other arm. Towards waiting members of the Committee on the Polish side of the border. Cast-off's from Germany's Third Reich. Jews.

With this group came Ruth Sorel, founder of a celebrated, world-famous dance school in Berlin, pupil of Mary Wigman in London. Almost immediately she received an honorary Polish citizenship and a right to open a school. My friends, Halka and Wanda, became full-time students. I joined two years later for the twice a week, hour-long workouts. That's where I met Flora.

She was easy to notice. Easy to remember. Her dance class finished as mine went on. I was undressing while she was slipping into a hand-embroidered slip. Silk-stockinged feet fumbling under the bench for elegant pumps. Strange what one remembers ... I remember the straps of her *dessous*. I knew it must have come from France because of those straps. So fine — so thin. Had to be turned on a thread. "Hallo. Hallo," we said twice a week, smiling at each other. The extent of our acquaintance.

Within a group of young, carefully educated, well-to-do and exquisitely groomed matrons, she was unique. She worked. She was a lawyer. A practicing lawyer. Prominent, because in the mid-twenties to early thirties she was the only one. A trailblazer. An original. Even to look at her — full of purpose, energy, vitality and good looking to boot. Someone like her needed only to BE. No more. But she was more. She had fantasy. Imagination. For instance, she had a shoemaker teach her to make ladies' sandals because those available were not to her liking. Or, those dance lessons at Ruth Sorel's school for professionals .... She could have had a masseuse come to her home instead, like her friends did ... but no ...

At Café Maurrizzio, during lunch break, she sat at tables reserved for judges, lawyers. Laughing, gossiping with those men. On equal footing. Relaxed. Totally emancipated. Passing the Café, still a teenager in my school uniform, I saw her. Through the frosted plate-glass window. Are you asking if she was married? Yes, of course! Such a catch! To a ne'er-do-well of a prominent family. A man-about-town. So that was Flora during my last school years. After matriculation, I left. Lost track of her.

1939. The unspeakable happened. War. I don't know how she fared during those tragic, grim years. But in the meantime we all were under occupation. Had to live. My apartment in Warsaw bulged with people. Near and dear ones. Those who could not reach their own apartments slept on makeshift beds, on floors all over. My friend Halka came as well.
"I have Ruth's address, we must visit her."
"Fine." I said, "Is she alone?"
"No, HE is with her."
"Again?" I was astonished. "What a crazy marriage! What a crazy couple! You remember how they almost killed each other? Then after the divorce, came together again, living happily after?"
"Yes, Choromanski is with her now and they are married again."
"Amazing!"
"You remember how he, the most celebrated writer, came down to the level of libretto writing for her school's presentation of The Seven Deadly Sins? How sparks flew? Their instantaneous love-hate-love relationship. Fascinating to observe. And spicy! There was George Groke, her leading man, mixed in as well, but we girls did not believe in this gossip. Did we?"
"Nonsense, we said."
"So she is here now ..."
We went visiting, bearing gifts. A tin of French sardines. One of the few left in my almost empty larder. A fistful of sugar cubes wrapped in a paper napkin. And here was Ruth in the rented room. On the sofa. Covered with a warm shawl. Dozing. One arm thrown back behind her narrow, blond head. Hair pulled tight into a chignon. Profile sharp against dark material.
"Where is Choromanski?"
"Oh, he went with my gold watch. To hock it. Hope he can buy some food .... Oh, sugar, how nice, I will have a cube right now. Thank you, it will do me good."

She was famished. But then, who wasn't hungry at this time in Warsaw?

Flora survived. How? I don't know. I heard that a relative (imagine, what a relative! a mogul in the film world of Hollywood!) fished her out of Poland in the 1950's. Brought her and her mother to New York. Where was her husband? He vanished. Like a hundred thousand others vanished. Anyway, she fitted the city like a hand in a glove. Saks Fifth Avenue offered her a job on sight. Promoted within a few weeks to buyer. One day I dropped in to say hello, and there she stood, with her back to me. About fifty steps away, but unmistakably Flora. In one of those little navy dresses. A French tricolor silk scarf negligently knotted. Hair carefully coifed. Making me feel a whit inadequate (need to check the seams of my stockings — are they straight?). This sort of feeling. A kiss. A hug.

"Imagine, you're here!"

"Oh yes. I'm quite all right. As you see. Mother? Oh, she's fine. Installed in our nice mid-Manhattan apartment. No, not alone. I was lucky to be able to arrange for a lady housekeeper. She spoils us both rotten. Lunch? No, Mother does not like to go out much. Dinner?... How true, you don't live here. Sure, I do have friends. Very good, nice friends."

And so we chatted. All was well with Flora.

Again, years passed. My years filled with life-building here in Montreal. Preoccupied. Then I heard some astonishing news. Here a shred. There a line. For it to make sense I had to pull all of it together. It appears that one day Flora spotted a wizened old woman. Corner of 38th Street. Rags on rags. Bulging shopping bags. At first Flora did not pay much attention. After all, she thought, this is New York. All sorts of strange people on the streets of New York. But this woman happened to usurp a particular spot around Saks day after day. Flora could not help but take notice. Even confided in her housekeeper. She became more curious. Intrigued. Spoke about it to her mother. Wondering. What is the woman doing there? Why? I have to see her better. And she passed a bit closer. Almost face to face. No, she is not old .... More my age. Flora became fascinated. Pulled, gossips said, as if by a magnet. Her eyes kept going to the huddled form. Is she waiting? No, not waiting. Each day seemed to reveal to Flora a new snippet of information. Is she unhappy? No. No, I don't think so. I would feel it. She mumbles to herself. Is she crazy? Lots of people mumble to themselves — so what? She is not crazy. Right. She smiles to herself, as if she is keeping a secret. She even laughs. Why? At us? Yes, she laughs at us! She thumbs her nose at all of us here on the street. Rushing. Rushing where? To work. Somewhere. From work. Nowhere. Why do we do it? Why do I do it? She is not rushing. How come she seems to be at peace? She must know something I do not know. What is her secret? Could she just be coping, simply coping with her life, the only way she knows how? Is that it? A person within her own world, a capsule. Complete. Why do I feel so close to her? Is she my mirror image?

And so it happened. One morning Flora stopped short before crossing the portals of Saks Fifth Avenue. Stood for a while. For a minute. Maybe longer. Did anyone see her do that? Then she turned away. Towards the street. And proceeded. At first uncertain. Slowly. Then with a brisk step. Sure.

She came home very late. With bruised feet.

"For God's sake — where were you? It's so late ... we were worried ..."

Next morning, before the two ladies woke up, Flora sneaked out. Old comfortable shoes on sore feet. Did not come back for the night. The two ladies phoned friends, police, were beside themselves with worry. She did not come home the next night either. Materialized days later. Warded off Mother.

"Please, Mummy, leave me alone, leave me be. I'm going to sign cheques. Here, to the housekeeper. Take these," and handed over a pile of bank slips. "I came to have a bath," she said. "If you want to see me from time to time, do not ask questions. Leave me alone." And that's how it was from then on. Flora kept her house key. Dropped in for a bath now and then. Soon barely resembled herself. Hair long. Scraggly. Grey. Wrinkled skin. Dried out. She smelled bad. She shrank. She became like the bag lady on the corner of 38th Street.

For herself she chose the belly-button of the Western World. Times Square. There she had her spot. All to herself, I was told. Among the milling crowd. Anonymous.

Time passed. Suddenly, one evening, I saw Ruth Sorel at a party. Here. In Montreal. Is it possible? When did she come? Does she live here?

She stood across the room. Surrounded by people. Did not look my way. Or did she? When I saw her leaving, I went over.

"Do you remember me? A friend of Halka? Wanda? Flora? Do you remember them?"

Her eyes a blank.

"Your company's production of The Seven Deadly Sins? Wanda danced "Pride." Do you remember that? Or Warsaw? Or the war?..."

Her eyes-evading. Inward looking. Told me nothing. But a thin, long, white arm out of the dark folds, waved above her head a disparaging dance gesture.

"It was so long ago ..." she said.

Turned her head to pale, sharp profile and with a swish of black cape, stepped out the door.

Later, on business in New York, I found Flora. When I came up to her she backed away. Her eyes told me she knew me.

"Flora," I said, "I spent ages trying to find you."

Her eyes became angry. She stepped back again.

"Don't you know me?"

Her feet shuffled with tiny steps. Running in place. Getting ready for flight. She cried,

"Nononono! — NO!"

I knew that any second she would really start running away.

"Flora, please, stop, don't run away."

But she, in mortal fear, eyes wild, skinny arm out of the frayed sleeve like a dried twig, waved the air in front of my face.

"Go away! I don't know you — go! Go! Go!" she shouted, "Apage Satanas!"

ANNA

She took the bus. Cheaper that way. Eight — nine hours. So what? Time did not matter. The old lady napped. Swayed in her seat. Much too large for her 83-year-old frame. Nowadays she slept lightly. Dreamt. Woke up. Dreamt again. Her thoughts shifted. With a secretive smile on pale lips. How not to smile? How not to feel happy?

In her mind she was back in Paris. Stan next to her. In the courtyard of the Sorbonne. Holding hands. Looking into each other's eyes. And laughing. They seemed to laugh most of the time. Even when hungry. Which was almost always. Hungry. Bless the French. Bless the *baguette*. Bless the *pain à discrétion* rule in small eateries on the Left Bank. Every restaurant had a basket full of cut-up, fresh, crusty *baguette* on tables. Salt and pepper. And mustard. One sat down and before a waiter materialized, ate of the bread. Bread with mustard. Bread without mustard. Bread sprinkled with salt. The waiters knew. *Le patron* knew. Students. Poor. Hungry. But here, in rich France, even foreigners should not go hungry. There is enough bread for everybody. The restaurateurs shook their heads. It would be a sin. And the students were allowed to come and leave at will. The owners also knew that as soon as money trickled in the same young people would be back. At the same tables. Ordering full meals. Waiters smiling. *Le patron* smiling. Oh, those sweet years in Paris...

The bus lurched. Woke her up. Never mind. It was convenient to board it in the middle of Manhattan and alight in downtown Montreal. Sometimes, book in hand, she read. Or looked out the window. She nibbled on buttered bread out of a brown paper bag. Dozed some more. And time passed. Sometimes she pored over a scientific paper about to be translated. She liked to do it. It tested her mettle, her memory. English into French. Or Polish. Russian into English. Or German. It brought much needed money. Whatever it was, came in handy. She smiled when the dictionary confirmed a word she already committed to paper. From her satchel she took out an apple and, with satisfaction, bit into it with still sharp, age-browned teeth. And slept again.

Twice-yearly she made this trip. Always in winter. Found summer travelling too hot. Inconvenient. But go, she must. It was necessary. She lived in New York but home was the Fulford house in the Eastern Townships. That's where she lived the longest with her love, her husband. The best times. How many years back? — when did he die? For goodness sake! How could she forget? It was more than 20 years now — yes — more than that. This, the last house they shared. The most beloved. She had to come here for a day or two. To give her strength. To assert her love. Year after year after year. It gave her soul nourishment. Peace.

The bus arrived well into evening. She put a coin into the telephone. Called one of her old friends still alive in Montreal.

"May I come over for tonight?"

"Sure. You're welcome. Come over."

In the morning Anna took a taxi to the bus depôt again. F r a local to the Eastern Townships. Light on her feet. Frail. Someho she didn't feel tired. Maybe because lately she was always tired? aybe because she was nearing her home? Like a horse close to it's s ole .... How well she knew this road. Granby. This turn. That tur Alot of travelling. But almost home.

At the General Store in Fulford she had to look sha for a lift. It might be somebody taking the dirt road to Knowlto Or Farmer Williams. Her nearest neighbour. Or even a taxi miraculo ly returning.

Let down in front of the old gate, she made h way gingerly through accumulated snow on the sagging veranda. o the kitchen door. The key fitted. It always did. And she smiled. Clammy, unventilated cold. Matches where she last left them. It took a few to light the kindling. She banked it slowly. Carefully. Checked the pipe. Yes. The warmth was rising. To the room directly above. To Stan's room. She shivered thinking of the penetrating chill in the other bedrooms.

Now, across the dirt road, down a quarter mile, close to the Yamaska river. To get a quart of milk from Farmer Williams' wife. The rest of her food brought in the cloth satchel.

Not at all like when they both lived on the Left Bank in Paris. With the bidet in their bedroom. Or in Chelsea, London. Narrow house, three floors up. Then, they could afford to go skiing. At home. In the Tatra mountains. The cold, bracing air. Talking of immortality.

Of the expanding universe. New, liberalising thoughts. Thrilling. Her Stan deep into Sanskrit. Eastern beliefs. Dark valleys and sharp, sunny peaks provoked speculations. Roaming minds. Roaming skis. Before the advent of ski lifts. And back to England. London, with its eternal drizzle. Hot mugfuls of dark, sweet, milky tea ...

Hm, life ... It was never as planned. Now, it's back to bare essentials. She didn't mind. Even felt gratified. Nothing changed here. A forgotten pocket where things remained as they were, she thought. Carefully avoiding muddy potholes. Hugging her milk bottle. If I fall and break a leg it could take hours till somebody spots me.

Mrs. Williams on the party-line to her friend.

"You know what? The crazy woman is back again. What do you mean asking, WHO? How many crazies do we have hereabouts? One is enough. Yes, as usual, for milk."

It takes a small place like Fulford. Anything can happen. By accident this call was intercepted on the Garage phone by one of the Wilburn brothers. And would you believe it? Farmer Williams was filling his diesel with petrol right then and there. It started them talking.

"That house is haunted, I tell you, for sure."

They guffawed. "Don't tell us. We know. We were with you. Fixing the wiring. Remember?"

"Yes, I do recall. It's haunted all right. The doors upstairs? Remember how they banged shut? Back and forth they banged."

"We could swear on the Bible, couldn't we?"

"There was nobody alive in that house."

"Only us."

"And we were downstairs. Nobody upstairs."

"Such a racket. You and your brother here, you both threw down the screwdrivers and you ran!"

"You, Williams, you were scared yourself!"

"True. I'll not deny it. When no living soul is in a house and doors start banging and banging away I say the house is haunted and I run. Once she asked me to fix the gate. I did. You know what she did when she came the next time? She slipped under the gate. Didn't even try to open it. Educated woman like that! They say she speaks seven languages. She is crazy for sure. To roll under a gate. In deep snow! A woman her age!"

Anna was getting ready for bed. With a hot water bottle, she went upstairs. The staircase lead from the kitchen into Stan's room. Small. Dark wood panelling. Womb like. Window framing the gently rolling countryside. The bed hard. Thinly camouflaged planks. They called each other Cat. Not kitten, or pussycat — no. Cat. She, settling down:

"Oh, Cat, how you always surprised me. The way you liked to "mortify" flesh. Your bed here. Rock hard. With your scientific background, your mathematics and engineering degrees, I guess metaphysics refreshed and amused you. Ah! Here you are, Cat! How happy it makes me to see you! Do I need to tell you? No. You know."

The apparition was visible to her. Checkered flannel shirt, thinning light hair, slightly ironic smile. Here he was. Her Cat. Her Stan.

"Yes, don't worry. I'm fine.

I didn't forget your scarf. This time I'm wearing it. Yes, it's cosy, warm. Sure I remember. Your Christmas present. Our first year in Canada.

Not here, I left it downstairs. Don't fuss. I have to tell you some things — tried to get back to the past when we were climbing in the Tatra mountains. I remember ME in plus fours! Heavy boots and woollen knee-high socks from Scotland. Sitting on a ledge, my feet dangling over a precipice. How well I recall it! Oh Cat, we were so happy! What I learned from you still sustains me. To you everything was simple. Even death. You taught me not to be afraid of death. I'm sorry to have to admit — you must know it — that deep inside me, I still am.

You were so wise. Don't pretend. You are laughing again. Making fun of me . . . Let me look at you. This time you are younger. Not bald, merely balding. I think I remember you better this way...

You're right, it's unimportant.

If you need to know — not too bad. My room, I told you, very comfortable. Near to everything. The Magazine gives me enough work.

You are fussing again. Not too much, I said, just enough.

Yes. I do see. People we used to know together. Stop asking silly questions....Cat, I miss you. I'll never stop missing you. We didn't tell each other, "I love you, I love you." But, it's not good for me to be without you. It's like there is only half of me. And it hurts like hell. Like after an amputation. One feels the cut off limb. Remember this house full of American ladies? Your pupils. And I was jealous ... so jealous ...

Don't! It's offending when you say it. I was never "the little wife". We both know I had plenty of grounds! Too late for this pussyfooting — I was insane with jealousy! Did you realize it? You helped me to whitewash the chicken-coop. And I moved out there. I wanted you out. Out of my life. But then I realized. It's not your body.

Or my body. What we were, what we are still to each other is much more. Cat, I miss you. I can hardly carry on without you...

No. Don't. I'll start crying. Don't say that. I don't want to cry. Not here. Not now. Let's stop.

Listen to us, Cat! Imagine somebody, anybody who would come into this room. Now. Would see me talking to a blank wall! Ha. Ha. They would send me straight to a lunatic asylum.

I'm glad it amuses you, too. Don't go. I'll close my eyes. I'm a little tired. I'll fall asleep with you near me. Stay a while longer. Stay."

She fell asleep. With a start, woke. Sat up. Sweatered shoulders from under the blanket exposed to the cold.

"No, Cat! You can't mean it! You can't be serious! I'm healthy! Nothing will happen to me. I will not stop coming here! How could I survive without talking to you? Your spirit's here. It's only here. I swear it's not hard on me. I can travel. Please, stay, stay."

A frigid breeze whisked her cheek. The room grew suddenly icy. Felt empty. She knew it was empty. And it would stay empty. She fell back against the pillow. Pulled the blanket over her head. Her thin body shaking. Racked with dry sobs.

Miss Mullins, the county's real estate agent, decided the day was nice enough. Snow melting. One could feel spring coming. Soon business should pick up. She took the side road. Stopped her car in front of the gently swinging gate. "Tsk, tsk," she clacked her tongue disapprovingly. Secured the gate properly with a wooden wedge. Definitely not happy with the way this property was maintained. The chicken coop needed a fresh coat of paint. Williams could do it. The funny little guest house had a broken window. Easy to replace. And the sagging veranda needed propping up! The Wilburn brothers could fix that job. No more visible repairs needed. It's a miracle. Shook her head. No going away from it — this is an abandoned house. Absent ownership. I don't even know her. Lives somewhere in New York. She should have put it on the market ages ago. While muttering to herself she took a neat little hammer out of her coat pocket. With deft, sure tap-taps she meticulously nailed up the cardboard sign. Right in the center of the gate-supporting two-by-four.

THIS PROPERTY FOR SALE

IRKA AND HALKA

Was I glad to see her across the room!!! First day in school and I had tons of news to tell her. Pushing girls out of the way we run towards each other. Linking elbows. Heads together. She, rushing her news right into my ear.

"I met this man!!!"

Taken aback — my summer highlights vanish. This was news.

"A boy?"

"No, not a boy — a man I tell you."

"What do you mean "a man"? Where did you meet him? Who is he?"

"Listen, listen — he is a university student. In Brno."

Gushing words trip over each other.

"Finished his second year of architecture. He is a grownup!!!"

"Is he gorgeous! Don't ask. He is divine — I tell you! You know what? He is an Olympic swimmer — a champion — that's where I met him — at the Olympic Pool in Bielsko. My Ernst — he is out of this world — and ... we are in love!!!"

I was speechless. Compared to this I did not even have a summer vacation. This was stupendous.

"You are in love? How do you know he loves you? — did he tell you?"

"Of course, he told me, you ninny! We kissed."

"What? You kissed him?"

"No! — it's not that I kissed him!! We kissed. It's not the same. He pushed his tongue into my mouth."

"Pfui, that's terrible. That's awful. I don't believe you."

"It's divine, silly. You don't know nothing. Wait till I tell you. It's a blessed feeling. And then — you know, his member got hard."

"What? What member? You mean his penis? Why? What do you mean "hard"?"

"Of course his penis, you idiot. Why hard? Because!!!"

"How hard?"

"Like wood."

"You're making it up. You're lying."

"No I'm not!"

"I don't believe you. It's idiotic."

"It's not. Listen — listen — don't be so stupid. One day you have to learn. That's how it is when one is in love. And don't tell me you don't believe me because I know and you don't!"

The bell. First bell for the first lesson of the new school year. We were the last in. Miss Piorkowna, our class mistress for the year, at our heels. Finger pointing at us.

"You two girls — do not even try to sit together. It will not work, not this year. You, first row under the window. You, second row near the door."

Halka still managed to whisper in my ear.

"It's my last year in school, next year I'm out."

Completely stupefied I sat where I was supposed to sit for the next ten months of classes, my mind a whirlpool, hardly conscious of what was going on around me. During this, Halka's last year in Gymnasium, we became even closer than before. Always together. We chose a whistle to summon each other for help when in trouble. And such was the intensity of dependence that it worked. Was it extrasensory perception? Who knows? But whatever it was, it worked. Not always, but it worked enough times for both of us to firmly believe that it was "always".

Every free afternoon, Sundays, holidays, we skied. I, dressed in a conventional manner, but Halka!! She was a sight to behold!! In heavy, knee-high, wool socks from Scotland, pleats of short, plaid skirt flying through Telemarks, Christianias. Jumps — never falling down. Her naked, partially-exposed thighs mottled blue from the extreme cold. Patiently waiting for me at the bottom of the hill. Our Tyroler felt hats sporting long, waving pheasant feathers. She was so much better than I was. Me, the abominable snowman.

During Easter school break, high in the mountains above the Valley of the Crocuses, dry cold dissipated in the blinding, brilliant heat of the sun. Parkas, sweaters off — in our bras we sunbathed. Stretched out on ski-pole propped-up skis. Eyes closed against intense glare.

Promising ourselves "forevers". Forevers...

Promising complete approval on the choice of boyfriends. Or else.

"How are we going to go about this? Give him up?"

"Simple. Drop him. What else? And no explanation needed."

Promising never to marry. Instead, each to choose the ideal man to father a child.

Promising to share house, possessions, everything. But above all, promising to have nothing to do with respective fathers of our two children. Such were our promises. Our forevers.

Late spring, before school's end, she again had fascinating news: "I have a paying job for the summer."

"You? A paying job? How did that happen?"

"Oh, it came by itself. I'm going to instruct swimming at the pool in Ustron, you know? The summer resort. A special class for little children. Even toddlers. It will be fun. Would you join me? I'll be paid. You're getting a little money. We could manage. How about it?"

"Would I join you? What a question!!! Wild horses could not keep me away."

I would have sold my soul to be with her and I knew Ustron well. That's where Grandma used to "hold court" some summers. In a secluded villa.

The municipal swimming pool was super olympic size. It had a large 200 foot terrace with a piano. Masses of kids hanging around.

"Yes, yes, I'm coming. Even if mother won't allow it."

We rented a room above a photographer's studio. A small square box of a house. Near the pond with rowing boats for rent. Downstairs, the studio. Above, the room with two dormer windows, a huge double bed, table and two chairs. That's what we rented. It had no staircase. Instead, from a minuscule entrance cubicle inside, a ladder. A pretty steep, wooden ladder and no handrails. Leading up to a trapdoor set in a wall. Electricity, yes, we had that. Water, no, this we did not have. A makeshift bathroom but no water. From the nearby well we lugged it in buckets up this ladder. No cupboards, but between the dormers three sets of built-in open shelves.

When our monies came in, first off, we went for a gut-bursting dinner, after which we bought absolute necessities like bread and tobacco. Of course we smoked. What a question!! Weren't we almost grownup? Not much smoking, mind you. It did not go well with swimming. The rest of our income got changed into coins. Standing away in the corner we alternated flinging it by fistfuls among the shelves.

"You, now, it's your turn."

"Now, let me."

Till we disposed of all the coins. Between then and the next financial deliverance we were rummaging amongst socks, blouses and shorts in dramatic suspense searching for money to buy bread.

Morning till dusk at the pool. Halka had a special gift teaching children.

"Do I swim well?"

"You swim perfect, like Archimedes."

"Was he a good swimmer?"

"Yes, he was and he was a famous man as well."

"Mommie, Mommie I swim like Archimes!"

First day off. We took a train to Bielsko.

"You absolutely must meet Ernst. At last, the two most important people in my world will come together. I wish you would approve of him. I hope you'll like him ..."

Up and down the hilly streets of the city. "Oh, look, look, those lovely shoes!"

Poised in the shop window. Black pumps on very high heels. Gros-grain bow at the vamp. "Those high heels are a dream. Mother would never allow for that." I wanted them. Badly.

"Get them."

"No, we can't afford them."

"Nonsense. We can. Go in and get them."

"You mean it?"

"Of course I mean it!!"

I walked out wearing the pumps. Halka carrying the shoebox with the old ones under her arm. And I? Looking down every minute to make sure pretty bows were still there. At the coffeehouse she phoned Ernst. We sat on the terrace looking down at people passing by — very content. Frozen Coffee came in tall, tulip glasses. At the bottom, rum-spiked black coffee, and on the top, a mountain of whipped cream. Heavenly. Life was dreamy. Admiring my new shoes sticking out from under the table. Happy.

Then Ernst came. Very handsome. I did expect a good looking fellow. Here he was. Swimmer's body. White summer shirt, open-necked. Relaxed. Laid back. We chatted about this and that. How unfair to have to cram during summer break to keep up with one's studies and so on. He was okay I approved. I liked him.

"Heavens, look at the hour! It's getting late. We better run if we want to catch the train!!!"

We made it just in time. Halka scrambled up the train steps. Still on the platform, we shook hands. He looked at me. Sort of funny. His eyes different. Questioning? Maybe, I don't know. Was I embarrassed? We shook hands awkwardly once more.

"Yes, you certainly have to visit with us ... come to Ustron ..."

Halka, with the shoebox, leaning out the open window.

"Hey, you two, hurry up!"

Then the train started to move — quite slow — I looked with surprise at the train steps gliding away. Halka madly waving her free hand from the window.

"You have the tickets in the purse. You have the money. I have no tickets — no tickets — no money!"

And before I knew what to do, what to shout back, the train passed the station, was beyond the bend. I became frantic. There must be one later on!! There was not. Unless one wanted to wait around till midnight. For the milktrain. The man behind the ticket window added:

"She stops at every station along the way, arrives early morning in Ustron. That's all there is on the timetable. Take it or leave it."

"No way. I can't wait, can't do it. She will be arrested. Have to go, have to rescue her. I have the bloody tickets. I have the purse. She will be jailed!!!"

"No, no, Irka. It's impossible to arrest somebody for an accident like this."

"Of course she can be arrested. It's you who does not understand, Ernst. How will they know it was an accident? They will think she wanted to cheat the railway."

Couldn't get it out of my head that THEY would hold Halka behind bars unless I appeared at the jail's door.

"Listen, Irka, I have an idea. It's still early. I know the way — we can walk across the mountain and be in Ustron hours before the train. Before sun-up."

"You mean it?"

"Sure. I know it. It's my mountain. I skied across it a hundred times, know all the shortcuts."

"But can you come? — with me? — now?"

"Of course I can. Wait here, I'll run home to tell Mother, pick up my ukulele. Meet you in 20 minutes."

We started to climb the grassy meadow with the sinking sun. My heels blistered. The new gorgeous shoes, off. Carried them in my hand. Oh, the bother! But the dewy, velvety grass, heaven under naked feet. Stupid shoes a deadweight. Darkness fell. No moon. Ernst strumming his ukulele. Singing *sotto voce* popular songs. His own songs.

"Do you know where we are? It's so dark — and the dogs…"

"Of course I know." Plucking his ukulele.

"Those barking dogs! Are they following us?"

"No way! We are skirting the houses."

"But they are barking all the time! I read there are some rabid ones loose — will they attack us?"

"Impossible. We are far away, going around the hamlets. Listen, I'll sing some more, and the moon will come out soon, you'll see. Soon, I promise."

"Ernst, do you really know where we are? I can hardly see in front of me and I'm tired, tired."

Climbing, still climbing. If I could only chuck away the shoes.

At last, above the treetops the moon came out. Sky grayed.

"I promised. Now you see? It's not far, we are almost there."

"Not far? How far is not far? When…"

"Soon. Soon."

Sky paled. Too tired to feel my legs, My feet moved on their own. And the shoes, if I could only throw away the shoes.

"Look, here we start down the mountain. Didn't I tell you it's not far?"

Sky, celadon streaked. Horizon appeared. And down below, a ribbon of asphalt road a short run away. We were at the jail in no time.

"You wait here, Ernst, I'll walk around and whistle and if she is in there — anywhere — she will whistle back and I will hear her."

But she did not, because she was not. She was home where we found her, asleep. She made room for us when we collapsed across the bed. Asleep at once. Still, even asleep I felt Ernst toss and turn between us. We breakfasted late on sardines and jam. I did not even notice that Ernst had brought a camera with him.

"I'll take some shots of those famous shoes. On your feet of course. If you will stand in a dormer against the light. All of your legs, that's it. Fine, Gorgeous. One more."

The usual photographer's patter.

He stayed the day. Everybody around the pool noticed when he dived. Breast skimming the surface, barely rippling the water. Powerful strokes, silky smooth. Looked almost lazy, effortless. Later, when summer people dribbled away for homes, we girls and a bunch of friends gathered around the piano on the veranda. Ukulele aside, Ernst played and sang for us his own compositions. He left for home before dark.

Years passed. Then the war. Our world fell apart never to be whole again.

Eons later. Living in Canada.

On one of my business trips to Europe. Dinner party at my school chum, Lilka's, house in London.

"Do you remember Ernst? Halka's famous boyfriend?" (Explaining to the other guests) "An Olympic champion swimmer, we all knew about him, sports-minded bunch that we were." She turned back to me: "You know he lives here in London now? For years. Well-established architect. Wife, two daughters. You know, the usual. You should call him."

"Should I?"

"Yes, you should. He would be glad to hear from Halka's best friend."

"How is it you are so well informed about him?"

"Oh, didn't you know? Stefan here is his solicitor. Aren't you, dear?"

At which moment her husband went to the hidden wall-safe, took out an envelope, and from it a harmonica-folded strip of paper. Handed it to me.

"Look at this," he said, with a supercilious smile.

I unfolded it. Photographs ... My Ustron photographs. Beautifully mounted. In a row. Under each picture a short, hand-penned poem. The other guests must have been quite mystified when I raised my voice:

"Those are my legs, my shoes. These photographs are mine, you have no right to own them. How did you come by them? How?"

Mitigated by the astonishment on the faces around me I stopped short, accepted Stefan's explanations. Something about a complicated court case for which he demanded this folder as an extra payment. And got it.

Next day, Sunday, as early as decently permissible, I did phone. A woman's voice answered.

"It's for you, she says an old friend..."

"Ernstl?" I pronounced his name the old way.

A long pause. And then without a moment's hesitation, "Irka, where are you? I'm coming to fetch you."

I was staying then at Yolanda's house. Poor thing, in the middle of a nervous breakdown, had her friend, Pipa, playing nurse-maid.

"Girls? How long will it take to drive over from Hampstead? Time enough for me to tell you a story? While I'm making up my face do you want to hear about this tiny little crush I had? And he, a friend of my best friend. We girls were teen-agers — can you imagine how long ago that was? Ages. I phoned him just now and he recognised me right after I pronounced his name. How silly can one be? I'm an old cow, a wife, a mother, a businesswoman. Still, I'm excited. As excited as he sounded. Memories coming from way back in the past. Sweet, innocent memories of twenty-four hours. When actually nothing happened. Only an idea. A feeling. Nebulous, distant, fleeting. An expectation of romance. A longing for love."

And I told them the story. Ending just when the doorbell rang.

"Pipa, dear, let him in, it must be Ernst. Come back and tell me..."

She came back with tears in her eyes.

"Oh Irka, such a sweet old gentleman..."

Then, in the car:

"Would you have recognised me in the street?"

"No, never."

"I wouldn't either. What a golden summer it was. It seems without a single rainy day. How young we were ..."

"Yes, young. But we shouldn't say it. It makes it sound banal, and it was not. Anything but banal."

"You don't know that the following winter I came to Krakow? Yes, I did. I felt I must see you again. Just once. Not even to speak to. Just to see you. I stood across the street watching your school. You came out with a bunch of girls. But you looked different. Not the same Irka. You were grey. The day was grey. Where was the sparkle? Where was the color? You were not the girl I would have even noticed. I went instantly back to Brno. Tried to forget. I did. Put it aside. Way back aside. Remembering only those brief, twenty-four summer hours. Do you realize we did not even hold hands?"

We drove in silence, which I interrupted:

"Now, Ernstl, you have some heavy explaining to do. Why did you hand over my photographs to Stefan? He is such a sleaze ... How could you do such a thing? How could you? To him of all people!"

"It was a terrible thing to do, I know. My weak moment. I don't know why. I can't explain. I'm a weak man. That's my only explanation. I thought, I'll never see you. Never. But I remembered you too well even without the photographs. Didn't have a chance to look at them for years. So I gave them away."

"To Stefan, to this worm? He wanted to kiss me. He bragged he almost did. Slanderer!"

"He insisted. After he won my court case, I gave in. And can't forgive myself..."

After a long pause, we arrived.

I looked around the house:

"Those wondrous sculptures — are they yours?"

"Yes, they are mine."

"And are you still composing songs?"

"No, I'm not composing songs anymore."

We were deep-seated in the livingroom around the huge, low table when his wife appeared. Handsome, tall woman, dark haired and sizing me up critically, from head to toe.

"Let me see you. Let me see the woman my husband carried a torch for all his life. Want to know what I see? I see a woman like we all are. A middle-aged woman."

LADY PENELOPE

Above the frothy peignoir's *décolletage* her shoulders shine like mother of pearl. She picks up a swan's down powder-puff, lightly dusts her warm flesh, shamelessly enjoying the touch of the feathers. Admires her own beauty.

"Yes, I'm beautiful. I like being beautiful. Let others be clever, smart — I do not care to be like them. I like being ME..."

Turns her delicate oval face at the discreet knock on the door. "Oh, Nanny? Is that you? Come in."

Fresh-faced, ruddy-cheeked girl leads in the twins, dressed identically in gingham frocks. They let go of her restraining hands and run to embrace Mother.

"Careful! Be careful!"

Lady Penelope genuinely likes her daughters. So sweet. So good. But at times like this, when she concentrates on her face or body, their presence is not welcome. Powder box almost upset!!! What a nuisance! She kisses them perfunctorily. Allowing little round arms to hug her.

"All right, all right — run along now, or you will be late for the Park. Mummy must get dressed."

They do remind her of Lord P., her husband. Somehow managing to jar her out of her moods. Like now. Just like him. He, kissing her too lightly. Or too abruptly. Or out of turn. Well, husbands! What was to be expected from husbands? But the painter, for instance! A shiver runs down her spine. That painter is different. So rugged. So foreign. I can read his face. He eats me with his eyes. I feel it. One more pronounced shiver down her spine. I like that. Today he comes again. Good. Another sitting. I do not mind how many he needs. I can easily lead him on. Too amusing, too exciting for words. How lovely to be beautiful. How beautiful to be lovely! She strokes her arm with elegant fingertips. Caressing the smooth flesh. "It's like satin," she smiles to herself.

The painter's a famous artist. Paints only beautiful women. Fees demanded in guineas automatically screen him from the common and reserve his talent for the rich and titled. In most cases, young. Their portraits to take their place and hang among those of Mothers, Grandmothers and other members of Family in home galleries. Pictures painted by Gainsborough, Reynolds and other titans of the craft.

It was whispered in drawing rooms — only among the closest of friends — that he was sleeping with his models. With all of them? Nay, only with the most beautiful. But they are all outstanding beauties! That's right. This accompanied by a dry, sarcastic chuckle. And it was true. He felt an enormous physical attraction to those slim, rosy-fleshed, long-torsoed females with delicate limbs and high-pitched birds' voices.

American women did not excite him that easily. Too strong. Too boyish. Those sporty, long-stemmed roses with raucous laughter.

Strangely, his amorous advances were hardly ever rebuked. And usually they started early, with the first or second sitting, ending amicably, sweetly, with the last. Nobody the wiser. For sure, all satisfied. Whispers? Yes, of course, but only whispers. Those were polite, well brought-up people who knew that it would serve no purpose to rake up the mud.

This particular case differed somewhat. This was the third sitting for Lady Penelope. Still nothing. The relationship stalled. Mischievious smiles, yes. Inviting twinkles from china-blue eyes, yes. But nothing else. Small coronet amidst the abundant, reddish blond hair. Rows of fabulous pearls nestling in the deep *décolletage* of the yellow satin gown, taking their pink glow from the famous peaches-and-cream complexion. She poses, straight-backed, on the antique settee. I wish I could see myself in a mirror. How do I look? Should I wear the same gown for the unveiling? How big should the party be? Have to make a list of guests. Oh, I wish I could see that I am as beautiful as I can be! After all, this is for ever and ever...me...to be seen by all the others...it is thrilling...

The next move comes from Lady Penelope. He is invited to a small dinner party in Belgravia and now awaits a weekend at the country estate, as is the custom. Instead, Lord P. phones suggesting a rendezvous at Club X for an afternoon's outing.

"Isn't that a nudist colony?"

"Yes, it is — do you mind? Lady Penelope and I thought it might amuse you."

"Yes, yes, of course. I would be delighted. I'd love to come."

The famous painter hardly sleeps the night before. He knows what to expect. Her young body under the shimmering silk holds but few secrets from his experienced eyes. Still, this might be a bold adventure. Because of this small uncertainty — how is he himself going to react? How is his body going to behave? After all, three weeks had already passed from the first sitting, three weeks of — one might call it — passion unsatisfied. Hopefully he could hold his own...

They meet at the gates where memberships are checked and only accompanied guests admitted. Soon after, they separate. Ladies to the right. Gentlemen to the left. Lady Penelope points to a spot, invisible behind lush shrubbery, farther down the path, where she will join them.

Impatient, he undresses first. Lord P. emerges and preceeds him down the sandy track among flowering bushes. On his pale, young body not a trace of a tan. And she? How will she be? She should be out any minute, appearing amongst those flowers. This 28-year-old beauty I long to possess. Where should I look first? I will look only at her face, into her eyes. Oh God, how I long for a towel, for a newspaper, for a hat. I will not be able to hide my shame.

Here she is. It's not too bad. I can hold on. Now she smiles. Only into her face. Look nowhere else. Now, mercifully, she turns her back, following her husband. I'm behind her. Now, I can feast my eyes! That swan's neck. Those slightly sloping, classical shoulders. Slowly... Slowly... this tapering, delicate torso. Slim, maidenly waist. I expected that much. Oh, no, I'm not disappointed, not at all! I'll let my eyes slide down towards those fabulous buttocks — round, firm, pale like a nacreus sea shell — satiny like a...

There was no need for a towel. For a hat. Or for a newspaper. From between those young, round, firm globes of Lady P.'s buttocks a triangle of toilet paper peeps out and moves with each step: left, right, left, right, left...

ALINE

I guess you would call them well-to-do. Above average well-to-do. Enough income to live in an excellent high-rise provided with a doorman. Retired. Enjoying the "golden years," the fruits of labours. Her name, Aline. To her friends, known as "Elegant Aline." His name, Harry. "Debonair Harry."

She was annoyed, due for her yearly medical check-up and disliking it thoroughly. "Ha, doctors! One goes in a well person — walks out sick. Or almost." She was right. "I'm always right," she thought when the doctor told her:

"Your blood pressure is way too high. I'll give you a prescription, but the best thing I can give you is advice. And my advice would be to walk. You have to walk."

"But I do walk! I walk now and I've walked all my life. In business I was on my feet all day long!"

"I don't mean that kind of walking. What I mean is wear proper walking shoes and move one foot in front of the other, at an even tempo, and for at least one hour. Rain or shine. And curb your appetite. I would like you to lose a few pounds in the process."

"But ... " she protested vigorously.

The "buts" flew back and forth. Eventually it was decided, by mutual consent, that Aline was going to walk every day. Including Sundays. That was a positive "yes." The second, the one about losing weight, was a decisive "no."

"I love eating. Have to have the pleasure of food. I'll never forget how hungry I was during the war. In Russia. Once gave a diamond ring for a loaf of bread. No dieting for me. Food stays. And, dear Doctor, I'll eat what I like when I like."

Every morning after that, the door opened for her by the doorman, Aline went out. And every morning she threw these departing words at him: "See you in two hours."

That's how it worked out. Two hours. Her route, east on Sherbrooke Street. One full hour. Sometimes so early that the city was just waking up. Washed fresh with the spring morning. Almost empty of passers-by. Before the rush for bus or metro. She was there. She was witness to the best hours Sherbrooke Street had to offer. The modern, glass-eyed high-rises blended with the old, venerable mansions. Mansions renovated into special offices like Corby's. The size of houses diminished with her progress farther and farther east. Became the quaint or ordinary Victorian dwellings of years gone by, until Sherbrooke Street changed character altogether and bore no resemblance to the large, tree-lined avenue of a rich city.

On adjoining streets, small businesses of all sorts. Eateries. Night clubs. Doorways painted crazy colors. St. Viateur Bagel Factory. Open twenty-four hours. Cars parked along the curb. Tail lights nudging headlights in an uninterrupted line. Between striptease joints, just about closed for the day, little restaurants, just about opening for early breakfast. A pedestrian rushing to work for an early shift. She loved it.

Looked at her watch. Almost an hour. Ten minutes more and *voilà!* Accomplished! Full of achievement, she went flushed and hot into the first restaurant at hand. Sat heavily at a table offering a street view. Ordered her breakfast. What a pleasure! To have done her walk and to indulge in a reward of freshly-brewed hot coffee and warm, crisp toast. Lots of butter and jam ordered in double portions. One cigarette before she had her steaming cup in front of her. The second cigarette with the last sips of the last cup. A ritual. A blessed ritual. She enjoyed it as if it was a divine repast.

Through the window she saw the number 24 bus approaching and crossed over in time to board it. She sometimes greeted the bus driver, recognized from a previous day, with a hearty, "Bonjour!" Arrived almost to the minute back in front of her apartment house, as she knew she would. The doorman greeted her: "Right on time, Madame."

She grew bored. Changed her route. Turned into side streets more often. Always going east, always ending up in a small eatery for breakfast. One day she ventured onto St. Lawrence Boulevard. Uphill, off Sherbrooke. By now, being an old veteran, walking was automatic and she didn't even feel the thoroughfare's up-swing. In front of Warszaw's Market, a bench. There was a bench near the *Banque Laurentienne* as well, but here the glass doors of the large grocery store swung open when her hour was just up.

So, well, I'll have breakfast a little later. It looks like fun around here. A man was sweeping a yawning entry to a dirty yard with an old-fashioned broom. Barrels were being unloaded. What's in them? Strange smells assaulted her nostrils. Herring? Salted herring? Pickles? And what else? She sat, her feet enjoying the rest.

Next to her was an old woman, looking like nothing more than a bundle of abandoned clothing. Head lowered, she seemed oblivious to her surroundings. She must belong here, thought Aline. It's probably her seat. I'm not in her way, am I? Aline took a packet of smokes from her purse. Putting a cigarette in her mouth, she took out one more and in her hand, offered it to the woman. Accepted without so much as a glance up. The old woman also accepted a light from Aline. Inhaled. Pushed herself farther away from Aline. Both sat. Smoked. After a few minutes Aline felt hungry. Where is my coffee? Well, that's that, I'm off to breakfast, she thought.

Next morning she took the same route. Again sat in front of "Warszaw's". The woman was already there, looking as she had the day before. A heap of rags. This time Aline extended the cigarette with the words, "Want a smoke?" Again, without a word, the woman accepted. Aline noticed her slim hand and her long, delicately tapered fingers. It looked to her like "class". But the filth! The stranger's hand was encrusted with dirt. Days-old, maybe even week-old dirt. Broken nails. Pfui, she thought. I could never take her home for a bath! What filth! Imagine, her whole body must be begrimed the same way. Pfui! Harry would throw me out. I could never do it. Pity. Great pity. Because I guess she's from the old country … she's an immigrant to Canada. Like me, I'm sure she was not born here. When did she arrive? Why did she let herself go this way? What happened to her? She could have even come from the same part of the world! Aline ventured a question:

"Are you from Europe?"

The woman turned her head and looked at her without interest. Exhaled a lungful of smoke.

"What's that to you?"

"Oh, nothing. I just thought I might have seen you before."

"No."

"Well then, I'm off. See you tomorrow."

Aline left, thinking, she can't be hungry. I know for sure that Warszaw gives away day or two-day-old food. So does Van Houtte. I know it for sure. So what's with her?

She felt a kinship with the stranger. Mentioned it to Harry. Told him in detail how the woman looked, how she behaved. Everything. But her husband just shook his head.

"You would like to befriend the whole world, wouldn't you?"

She kissed the top of his bald head. What a lovely man. Her Harry. Never mind their bickering. Sometimes in earnest. Sometimes in jest. Bantering. Over forty years, married! And she said, for the umpteenth time, "I'm lucky." Harry looked up from his newspaper.

"How did that come out now? I'll never understand how your mind works! What that's to do with everything else — I don't know! Bizarre!" and went back to his reading.

Aline's mind flashed back to the woman. Oh, how I would love to offer her a long, hot bath. And remembered her wild longing in Russia for a tubful of bath water.

Oh yes, she was lucky. In her retirement, to fill out the long hours without a work routine, she repainted damaged porcelain bought in so-called "antique" stores. Repaired broken china found in garage sales. Embroidered pictures. Knitted afghans she gave away as presents. Sewed blouses requiring only two side seams and a hole for the head to come through. She was busy, busy, busy all day long. By dinnertime she was almost falling off her feet. But, no, oh no, no rest!

She started her social "whirl". Dragged Harry for visits to friends. For tea and cake. For talk and gossip. Between ten and eleven at night, exhausted, they were both in bed. She, with a french *roman*, managed to read only for a few minutes before falling asleep, novel abandoned on the floor. Slept the sleep of the just. Until two in the morning when she woke up starving. She needed food. And a routine developed. Now it was time for her first breakfast of the day. She shook Harry's shoulder.

"Harry, dear love, I'm hungry."

He roused himself from a deep slumber. Sat up. Eyes barely open.

"Yes, yes, I know. So what will it be? The big one or the small one?" One day it was this one, the next, the other one. The big one consisted of rye bread, toasted golden brown with a layer of Swiss cheese, two slices of cake and coffee. The small one, just a toast or two with jam and the irresistable coffee. Harry brought it over from the kitchenette on a tray.

Back in bed he turned away from the light and immediately fell back to sleep. Aline read her *roman* for awhile. Then turned off the lamp and slept till six in the morning when she required her second breakfast. What would it be? It could be for instance, a Danish, nicely oven-warmed, or some coffeecake — crumble topped. Or maybe something else. And off she went. It was proverbial. Everybody knew it among their friends: Aline ate about eight times a day. Or more. And maintained her weight.

The woman on the bench in front of Warszaw's was on her mind. Why is it impossible to talk to her? Why does she turn her head away? Why does she move away from me on the bench? She doesn't want to be near me. Well, it's her right, not responding. Takes the stryofoam cup full of well-sugared milky coffee — that's all the response I get! Still, I must help her! I must do something for her. I know what! I'll start by giving her something to wear. Something of my own. My blouses. That's it! That'll be the beginning!

The blouses, fresh, folded beautifully, packed in a plastic Steinberg's shopping bag, were ready in Aline's purse to be given as presents.

I have so many ... I'm sure she can use them ... Later I'll try something more substantial to give. She'll soon need a winter coat. I have so many ...

Sitting on the bench, Aline did not look that much different from the old woman. Her old, nondescript walking coat — totally *demodé*. Felt hat pulled down. Round like a brimmed pot. Could be worn back to front and front to back. At first glance, not markedly different from the woman. So, it happened that next time, when just about to take her leave, Aline bent down to her roomy handbag leaning against the bench, took out the parcel and extended it to the woman.

"I have something here for you. It's mine. You might use it. Please."

The woman turned to face her with a steely gaze. Straightened her thin shoulders. Pursed her lips. Stood up. Bent towards Aline. Like a strange bird with an extended, stringy neck. And let out a stream of words:

"How dare you? Who gave you permission? You think I can't buy my own? You think I have no money? I have money! Plenty of money! I don't want you to give things to me! I don't want you talking to me! I don't want to see you! Go away from me! Go! And don't ever come near me!"

She turned away to pick up her bulging shopping bags and with a defiant back, walked briskly away.

Aline sat stunned. The plastic bag in her extended hand. Well! That was a lesson. That was something I'll never forget. Well, well ... I'll be darned!

Next day, persistent, thought, I'll try her out one last time. But the bench was empty. Aline sat alone for a while, watching the ragged old man sweeping the entrance to the decrepit warehouse. Felt cold. It's turning nippy. Autumn is upon us. The need for a cup of hot coffee overwhelmed her. I better go .... And left. Eh, I've had enough of the east side. I'll try the west tomorrow.

Along Sherbrooke, towards Claremont Street. New atmosphere. English Montreal. Same sort of small businesses. Fewer shoe stores. No "nudie" shops. Cafés. Murray's Restaurant. Fruit stores on ground floors of renovated apartment houses. Dog-grooming salons. And the same peace of early morning. She marched with a quicker step now that it turned cold. Walked back, instead of taking the 24 bus. Have to learn more about this part of town. Steinberg's already opened it's doors. Hey, there is an old man standing there!

Cap in hand, leaning against the wall. Next to the Royal Bank's entrance. Did I see him before? I think so. I'll buy him a cup of coffee. I need one myself. And she went up to the man. Dropped some coins into his cap. Extended a coffee towards him. Noted the drop hanging from his nose. He is cold! Immediately, long, hungry winter days in Russia flashed before her. She shivered. Well, thank God, that's over for me. Harry was skinny as a rail. And his Long Johns! I must still have them tucked away. They could do nicely for this man. Slacks? No, unless I take them in in the side seams. Yes, slimmer, they would do.

"Here, have some coffee. It's warm. Let's sit down here a while." She indicated the street bench. Tucked her flatheeled, tired feet under the bench against the chill, her head in a wool hat, which could be worn back to front and front to back. She turned towards the man:

"Are you a Montrealer?"

TRUDI

She snapped the suitcase shut, looked around the room. She was proud of her room. Nobody would have guessed the furniture belonged to her landlady. Nobody. Her own things, the pretty things, dominated. Colorful throws, little, playful, fancy pillows, flowered curtains and lots of pink, silk lamp shades. All feminine, soft, alluring. To make one feel at ease, lazy, relaxed. That was Trudi's aim. That's what she wanted. To make her nice, male visitors feel at home. Or more than at home. Her gentlemen callers. Let them feel special. She herself needed this decor after a day on her feet in the shoe store. She, also, needed to feel special.

Well, time to go. One more look around. Windows lifted a fraction for ventilation, kitchen faucets turned off smartly, gas pilot alight, all done. She closed the door firmly behind her. Suitcase in hand, she knocked at her neighbour's across the hall.

"Liselotte, I'm leaving now!"

A redhead of "certain age" opened a door to an exact replica of her own apartment. A replica without the frills. Just like Hamburg. Staid Hamburg. Liselotte didn't believe in frills. Had her own furniture. Solid. Old fashioned. Everything had to be utilitarian. Durable. Just right. That's what they taught her for her job in the post office. That's what she became. Dark, friendly appraising eyes looked Trudi up and down.

"You look super. But high heels for a bus trip?"

"Don't you understand? I might meet somebody. It's a long ride! By the way, if you run out of cognac I have a bottle of Martel in the cupboard and the Schnapps is in the freezer."

Liselotte laughed warmly. "You know I don't drink alone, you silly! Go. Go, you'll be late." They embraced warmly.

Liselotte tucked Trudi's apartment key under a flower pot. Went back to her cross-word puzzle, shaking her head.

"...that Trudi..." she said.

In the *Autocar* she settled comfortably. Looked around. Very disappointing. Not one promising male face. Not even one. Only dull German couples, like the ones who passed you in the streets of Hamburg. She decided, it's better to close my eyes. And fell asleep.

There were always four, five of them. All waiters from the Ritz. Spending their free time after having served lunch, before the next shift, with a glass of wine. On the terrace of the Bodega in front of the *Autocar*'s last stop. A table permanently reserved for them.

You had to be *some* waiter to be able to work at the Ritz. The most prestigious of all eating places in Barcelona. You had to know your craft. Be polite. Perfectly mannered. And memory. Memory? You had to remember absolutely everything. Who is who. Who likes what and in what form. Who is cheating on whom and with whom. Mixing up of names, an absolute no-no. And connections! Who was connected with whom. Be scrupulously "clean." If you cheated on your colleagues — ha! — you'd be finished. For ever. Life wouldn't be worth living. Money comes into your hand, it has to be divided to the penny. Clean means the entire body. Body means buffed fingernails, hands creamed before going to bed. Never mind how late it was and how tired you were. One had to be perfect. Our Manuel was as perfect as they come. The fact that he was of small stature, and walked sort of funny (like he had two left feet), the fact that when tired, he squinted, or the fact that his nose was a bit big for his face, all this didn't matter. He was well liked. What was more important and plainly visible, the Maître D' liked him best. There was no need to re-count the silver, re-check the number of wine bottles or how much Boursault came back on the cheese tray. One didn't need to do these things with Manuel.

It was well into the early evening. The time when humans came alive again. After "siesta." They say most babies are started during those early hours after an opulent lunch. During siesta time. Ha, that's how the world goes round.

Manuel wasn't married. His friends joshed him about it.

"Hey, Manuel, why aren't you married? You're getting old. Better do something about it."

"Ah, I look around — I find nobody right for me. I'll wait a while longer. She'll come along. Any day now. I'm not in any hurry." That's what he answered. "As long as I'm not getting bald — I'll find the right girl."

And he waited. But in his mind he knew what he waited for. An Angel. A blue-eyed, blond, full-bodied Angel. He didn't know exactly how she'd look. Face somehow shadowed. Invisible. But he knew that her eyes would be blue and her hair straw-coloured. Couldn't tell more about her, only that one day — BOOM! — she'd be there. Right in front of him. And he'd marry her.

In the meantime, everyday before a fresh wash and a new change of linen, before returning to his station at the Ritz, he sat there. On the terrace across from the *Autocar* Stop. His eyes peeled for those descending the three steps of the Bus. It came from Germany. He liked Germans. They treated you right. Gave good *pourboires*. Of course patrons of the Ritz didn't come in an *autocar*! Ha! That would be funny. No. They came in a more luxurious way. Still. He liked to watch who was coming by bus. Tourists from Hamburg, Berlin, Frankfurt or wherever. During this time, his time of luxury, he was served. He was brought a glass of wine. He had an ashtray put in front of him. HE was somebody. It felt good to be a patron. Not a servitor.

One day he saw HER. First he noticed a shapely ankle in a white sandal. High-heeled. The pedicured foot had bright-red, enamelled toenails. Wow! His eyes could notice in one second much more than somebody else who'd look for half an hour and notice nothing. After the slim ankle, a lovely rounded calf, short skirt — and something twinged in him. His stomach jumped. He knew that after the brightly coloured dress there would be a pair of blue eyes and a head of curly blond hair. He just knew it! It felt so in his stomach. That's his Angel. His back straightened up. He became fully alert.

It showed. "What's happened, Manuel?" they asked him. But he just stood up. Pushed his chair back and without a word started across the pavement towards the group of tourists milling around the huge vehicle. Waiting for their suitcases brought out from the belly of the car. Manuel didn't know what he'd say. Or do. He only knew he couldn't lose sight of his Angel. Yes, she did have blue eyes. Yes, she had curly blond hair. Yes, she was his Angel. He'd find a way to get her. Hurried steps took him over. She stood to the side of him. His left hand took out a pack of cigarettes. His right hand made a quick, minimal cross over his heart. For good luck.

"Fraulein, I speak German. Can I help?" He extended the cigarettes. His constricted chest managed one more sentence. "Would you like to smoke?" And waited.

She turned her head towards him. Eyes wary. Knowledgeable. Sized him up. That's when Manuel saw the wrinkles. Around blue eyes. Around painted lips. The slightly darker roots of blond hair. He saw it all. He could guess her age pretty well. But instead of dismay or disappointment this only released his tension. Relaxed him. Less frightened now because it made his Angel more approachable. His breath became normal. Yes, she was older. So what? Was he a youngster? Why should she be young? Still, she was beautiful. Dainty, small mouth. My Angel. I can see now, she's truly for me.

She sized him up. From head to toe. Saw his well-shined shoes. His polished nails. Lifted both eyebrows and, with a girlish smile touched with irony, "Yes," she said, "I'll gladly take a cigarette." Her teeth showed. You might say she challenged Manuel. And he, Manuel? He was enchanted! She took the cigarette. He provided the light. His hand firm. Astonished that it didn't shake, he wanted to pat his own shoulder approvingly. Good beginning!

"Could I help?" He repeated.

"I don't know. Could you? Could you get my suitcase right away? I'm a little tired."

This told Manuel quite a bit. It told him she was single. Travelling alone. And that he had made a favorable impression. Good. Good. Now to act swiftly. Those *autocars* brought people for two weeks. With side trips every day. How much time did he have? Not much.

With great authority, sure of his step after she pointed out which one belonged to her, he approached the driver. In German said, "I'll take that." At the curb, snapped his fingers at a cruising taxi. Opened the door and followed her inside, leaving the loading of the case to the taxi chauffeur. (Like he had been doing things this way all his life. Taking taxis. Ordering chauffeurs around.)

His friends across the street did not take their eyes off Manuel. "What's going on there? That's not the Manuel I know!"

"Where's he taking that woman?"

"What's he doing?"

Inside the taxi Manuel eased and lifted the crease of his trousers. Crossing legs as he'd seen relaxed gentlemen do. Asked, "Fraulein, can you give me the address of your hotel?" Sitting close because of the smallness of the taxi, she looked him in the face and so did he hers. Was handed over an excursion sheet of the trip from Hamburg. Gave the hotel's name to the driver. Didn't take his eyes off her smiling face, wrinkles and all.

"Fraulein, I think you are beautiful. I want to see you again. Could you have dinner with me tonight at the Ritz?" He astounded himself. What had he said? How could he have said it?

Her smile vanished. With wide open eyes she repeated, "At the Ritz?" Who is this man? I thought I knew men. I live off them. But this one? Who is he? I better keep him! You never know. You never can tell. "Yes, it will be my pleasure. My name is Trudi Deutsch. What's yours?"

Manuel calculated in his mind the consequences of what he had just said. What to do now? Santa Maria, Madre de Dio! What am I going to do? His mind in a whirl, he prayed fervently. While kissing Trudi's hand for "Adios," he reminded her, "In Spain, we eat late. Can I expect you at ten o'clock in the main dining room of the Ritz? I'm a waiter there."

It was done! He had said it! Now, only to think how. How to find a way.

His station in the main Salon was not too good and not too bad. True, he was a superb waiter, but because of his stature and his way of walking (like he had two left feet), he knew this was the best he could expect. He wasn't tall. He wasn't smashingly good looking like Pedro or Sebastian. He saw the way women looked at those two. Many times he saw bits of paper pushed into their palms by women — probably suggesting ways of assignations — he saw all that. But didn't complain. His *pourboires* were bigger than theirs. Because of his memory. He remembered all he was supposed to remember to make the patrons happy. And the men tipped. His station wasn't so fantastic — so what will Trudi think? Will the Maitre D' listen to his request? Questions. Questions. Madre de Dio, help me, Santa Madonna!

The Maitre D' looked at Manuel with astonishment. What an unusual request. First time anybody asked for such a favour.

"I didn't know you had a fiancée! When did that take place? Were there no festivities? And who is the lucky lady? Let me think, Manuel. Let me think one minute."

Manuel found the small round table himself in the pantry. Dressed it. Placed it where the Maitre D' indicated. Just near the wall. Not far from the kitchen entry. At the edge of his station. It was done. The cheque, to be deducted from Manuel's wages at the end of the week. He was happy. Waited.

She arrived at ten exactly. Dressed all in white. Blond hair fluffed up. Round eyed. The splendour of the Grand Salon! The gold trimmings! Gleaming crystal chandeliers! Flower arrangements! Waiters in tails. And this funny man, Manuel, greeting her with a bow. Leading her to the little table. It was too much.... She was overwhelmed.

Later, she had to wait for him in the vestibule. For his "mop-up," as he called it.

After the last guest left, the detailed order of the pantry restored, accounting done, he came out from behind a side door she hadn't even noticed.

When walking her back, he inquired, "And what are you doing when not vacationing?"

"I work in a department store. I'm in sales. The shoe department. Men's shoes."

"A lady selling men's shoes? That's unusual."

"I'm doing very well. I guess the buyers like a woman serving their feet. Who knows?" And here she allowed herself an unladylike remark: "Maybe they like to look down at my cleavage." And she laughed.

He was taken aback. Strange, what she said. But after all, she comes from a big, central European city, Hamburg. Things are different there.

They made an appointment for the next day. He insisted on seeing her.

"Look, Fraulein Trudi, I like you a lot. I want to know you. Never mind your side trips — I'll take you to the interesting places in Barcelona. I would like to spend all my free time with you."

She looked at him sharply. Mind racing. What is he aiming at? He looks serious. How serious is serious? He is an odd little man. Not so little, shouldn't say it even to myself — he's my height, almost. What has he got on his mind? Should I begin to treat him for real? He hints at all sorts of things — like he wants to take me out into the country to meet his mother. God in Heavens! Not one of my male friends ever said anything like that.

He continued. "The trouble is, I have only one day a week free. Friday. Could you give me all of your Friday?"

"But Friday is after tomorrow!"

"Yes, that's right. And tomorrow I am going to ask you to spend my siesta time with me. I can live without it and you can rest before. Then I go to work. You'll eat in the Bodega. I know, I'll take you there and you'll wait till I come to fetch you after work."

"Goodness gracious! You're arranging all my time." She smiled, her mind calculating how to deal with this completely new situation. "You're not even asking. You're just arranging my life. Should I let you do that?"

"Yes, you should. Because I'm serious about you. And I want you to know me, Manuel, better."

She interrupted.

"We just met ..."

Her mind was busy. Does he want me to live with him? No way. I'm going back to Hamburg. Why does he want me to meet his mother? That's when you want to marry somebody. No way! So what will it be? And she couldn't answer that. And then, like a flash, a thought: I'm not young any more. I'm getting on. Do I have a better future in Hamburg? To knock on Liselotte's door to make a foursome for an evening? Is that better? The thought vanished as it had come, in a flash. Suddenly she felt tired. Very tired. I'll let this go its own way. Who knows where it will take me?

She insisted on keeping one day free. To join the group she came with. He reluctantly agreed.

"I'll miss you. You know, you're the woman I dreamt about. I'm not joking. I'm too old to joke about a serious thing like this. Soon you might leave for Hamburg. I want to keep you here. Would you give me a chance? Don't take away one day of the few remaining."

He looked pitiful.

Gazing at his sorrowful eyes she thought about his funny walk, about this Barcelona which wasn't her city. Not like Hamburg. What was she going to do?

"I need to think about all of this. That's why I have to have a day to myself."

He could insist no more.

Actually, she didn't join her fellow tourists. She wandered around in the warm sunshine. Browsed in a store. Sat on a bench in the park. Thinking. And what would happen if she did agree to stay for a while? She might return home with the next excursion trip on the same route. It could be arranged. And what if... Curiously, she missed him. She missed his warmth, his adoring eyes. She missed him even more knowing she wouldn't see him in the evening. That's funny. I do like him, she concluded. He's not the man I dreamt about, still... Marriage? Is this going to become a love story? And why not? I could become a wife. I know how to cook, keep house... Why not? Let's try it. If he asks me again I'll move in with him for a day or two.

What do I risk? I'm risking a job of selling shoes to strange men. And once in a while — or, often — accepting invitations from some of them. Being paid for it. Getting old this way isn't much fun. My bank deposits won't keep me warm.

Manuel was an abstemious man. He did not demand much from life. He fervently hoped that this good-looking woman, identical to the future wife of his dream, would become his spouse. But when asked — would she? He paled.
Trudi expected it. She didn't pale.
"Manuel, ho-ho, don't be so quick! With me it doesn't work so quick. You see, that's why I'm still single. But, it's true I'm not getting any younger. You know what, I'm going to come to your place for the last three days. So how about it? We'll try it out. We'll see."
He hoped his trembling didn't show.

It was something to come home! To his modest home. Find lighted windows. His heart racing. From happiness. If she left him, went home, what would he do? Go back to the emptiness that was? The very thought was painful. He prayed fervently. "Let her stay, Santa Madonna, let her stay."

Work. An evening like the others. Everything just so. Perfect.
And then, the incident. Four tables away at Sebastian's station. A table for four. Two matrons and two young men. Relations? Lovers? Who knows. Anyway, there seemed to be an argument. Attack of jealousy? One of the ladies pushed the other. The other responded with a shove. Next came a punch in the shoulder and a ring got entangled in a magnificent necklace, a triple strand of pearls. The clasp must have opposed the forces of entanglement and the threads broke instead.
Necklace broken. Pearls spilling to the parquet floor. Voices of diners hushed to mute. A simultaneous cry of anguish from a female throat. One hand clasping a frightened mouth. The other holding the beating heart. All heads turning her way. All eyes following the cascading pearls. Ping. Ping. Ping. Ping. All over. And such a magnificent necklace. Ping. Ping. Huge pearls. Ping. Ping. Ping. Rolling. Towards the edges of the salon. Ping. Ping. Under tables caparisoned with long, heavy, damask cloths. Already hiding in deep folds, in dark corners. Ping.
Within seconds, all the waiters from all the stations were on the floor. On their knees. Crawling like so many black bugs. The tails of

their evening coats waving behind them with every move. Stillness broken with a hissed remark from behind clenched teeth. One of the two ladies — those nearby could hear it — said, "I told you a year ago, you stupid cow, to restring those pearls!"

Manuel, on all fours, like the others. Fully alert and eager to be of service. He dived under the nearest table and in the dimness of the sheltering tablecloth found a pool of beads coming to rest near a booted foot. He picked them up. One by one. Into the left hand's palm. All was still. Nobody spoke a word. Only the (by now) faint sound of rolling pearls. Manuel's eyes darted around. Six pairs of feet. Male and female. Nothing else. Nobody looking. Not a lowered face checking on him. Only shoes. He was safe. And without thinking, almost automatically, he put the last two beads in his mouth and swallowed. They went down. He crawled out from under the table. Quickly turned towards Sebastian's station. Put his handful of pearls on the table in front of the old lady. She, still holding on to her heart and her half-opened mouth. He, backing off with a proper bow.

He could almost feel the pearls going down. What he felt of course, was his own fright, not the pearls, settling in his stomach.

With lots of whisperings, the injured party left soon after. All the other guests went back to work with their forks and knives. All was almost normal. The evening ended.

Manuel started home. His feet heavy. His beautiful Trudi would be asleep. He wouldn't wake her. Their love-life was now over the first hurdle of two sexual encounters. Both at siesta time. The Spanish way. No. He wouldn't wake her. Slowly, he crept upstairs. In semi-darkness — light provided by the shining street lamp — he undressed. Small change from his trousers' pocket and keys deposited on the night table. Without any noise. Carefully. Once in bed he turned away from Trudi, not to wake her. Immediately he turned back towards her.

And so it went. Left and right. He was tossing and turning, trying not to disturb the woman sleeping soundly next to him. No. This will not do!

Delicately, with trembling fingers, he touched her naked shoulder. Whispered. "Trudi ... Trudi... "

She woke up. Turned her head half-way towards him. "What is it, Manuel?"

"I have to tell you something."

"Yes. So what is it?" Just a bit impatient.

He described the whole pearl incident in Sebastian's station. Ended by saying, "I swallowed two pearls."

"What?"

"I did. I swallowed two pearls to make a pair of earrings for your beautiful ears."

"What are you saying?" She, half-sitting up, resting on her elbows, with eyes full of astonishment and attention, turned to him. He, thinking how much he loved this woman, his Trudi.

"Yes." He repeated. "I swallowed two pearls to have earrings made for you."

From the half-sitting position, she sat up. Fully alert. "You have them in you, now? Inside?"

"Yes. In my belly."

"Oh, my God! And you did this for me? You, so painfully honest, you became a thief for me? For me? Trudi? Oh, my God! You love me! Manuel, you love me for sure!"

She jumped out. Stood at the foot of the bed facing him.

"I'm staying! Do you hear me? I'm staying with you!"

She started to laugh. Threw both her hands up from sheer wonderment. And cried out.

"The man loves me and I'm going to have pearl earrings! " And ran towards the kitchen.

She was still laughing when she came running back from the kitchen. In her hand, a sieve.

THREE LADIES

A beautiful, golden autumn day in Warsaw. Chestnut trees in full glory, lining the broad Allée in flaming colours. Air still balmy with a discreet promise of frost to come, but not yet ... not just yet .... A perfect *Shabat* day in the year 1936 when Roberta broke ranks.

She was second of the group. During dinner when the family sat around her table, when Marysia, her trusted cook, circled the festive board with laden dishes, offering her children, grandchildren, and sons-in-law second helpings. More roasted capon. More pudding. More vegetables. Big dinners were customary from the time her husband passed away. When was that? Oh, my goodness. More than three years. How time flies. That's when Marysia became almost a member of the family. But now, Roberta stopped her. With raised right palm.

"Marysia, it's enough. No more food. Enough of all that."

"But, Madame, Suzy wants more pudding."

"Never mind, Marysia. Leave us alone. Please. Go to the kitchen. Keep the cake and coffee until I ring the bell."

This exclusion was so unusual that Marysia became flustered. Forgot even to pout. Round-eyed, she scanned the equally astonished, familiar faces of the diners. Saw no visible support for her obvious rights and slowly turned around. With hands fully occupied her generously broad behind pushed the kitchen door open, swallowing her.

Seeing the family ready to attack her with questions, Roberta shushed them.

"Wait. I have something to announce. Ssh — ssh — ssh — let me speak. You can talk later. Do you remember my old school chum, Pauline? The one who moved away to visit with her two sons in the United States? Years ago it was ... anyway, I didn't know where she eventually ended up. Until last week. I got a letter from her. Imagine, she settled in Côte d'Azur! The letter was postmarked Nice. That's where she is now. It appears language and lack of friends was too much for her in America. She knows French like us. So the French Coast seemed a better choice. From the letter's contents, obviously better. I conclude from it that she's very happy in Nice. Anyway, she writes, 'wish you were here'. And you know something? I wish I was there.

"I've thought about it. And I've pondered it. Back and forth. Why am I here? What for? I'm not needed anymore. And thank God I'm not needed! You're so well off! In every respect. Once a week, together with Marysia, I cook up a storm. You all come here and we share the meal. Wonderful. The rest of the week, you phone. You phone me, my dear, dutiful daughters. Daily! Sometimes even a few times a day. Often enough, I'm not complaining! Don't get me wrong, you're busy. So busy that this is plenty of communication. But what about me? What am I doing all the time between calls? I'm waiting. Waiting. That's what I am doing. Waiting for next weekend.

"Do you think this is enough? No, it is not.

"Well, I decided. I'm moving to Nice. Let's see how I'll manage there among other widowed women. It seems there is quite a little bunch of old "birds" living on the Côte d'Azur. It might be less boring. Your faces show amazement. Yes, yes. I know you never imagined I might be bored with my life. But I am. Very bored. So now I said it, let me continue. Over there, on the Côte d'Azur I might paint. Or sit under palm trees. Or I might play cards with new friends. Imagine, shaded by a parasol! Or go to the Casino every evening. Or walk along the Promenade des Anglais looking at other people just like me. Who knows? Let me try it. Let me break out. You, frankly, don't need me here ... true?"

Her appraising eyes went around the astonished faces.

"Close your mouth, Fanny. Don't look at me that way. And you, Lenka, your eyes are as round as saucers. Sophie. I forbid you to cry! It's silly! Listen, if things don't work out as planned, I'll be back. Quick as the wind I'll be back here, among you all. So, cheer up!"

"But Mammy ..."

"But what if ..."

"Mother, for God's sake, why so sudden ..."

"Ma, I can't stand it, why so soon ..."

"All of you, relax! The old lady is breaking away. Sorry I could not have prepared you for this move, because I didn't know it myself. I hardly knew I was going to "announce" it this Saturday. But here you are! I did it! Of course you're surprised. Your loving, dutiful, secure-as-a-rock mother is breaking away. But I? I'm ready. Ready to go. No, my dear Sophie, not later. It's now. Now or never."

After a while, all possible angles of dissent were parried or rejected. Subdued, they looked disbelievingly at Roberta. The 'new' Roberta. So sure of herself. How, when, did all this happen? There must have been a strong current before Pauline's letter, thought Fanny, her oldest daughter.

Roberta rang the little silver bell. Marysia, with a stormy face and pursed lips, came in from the kitchen.

"Marysia, don't tell me you're against me as well? I know you eavesdropped. Never mind. I'll explain all this to you later when we're alone. Now, please, where is our dessert? And coffee?"

Marysia returned bearing an enormous torte. Surprise ending for each dinner. Followed by a tray of coffee cups and tea glasses. It was Fanny who poured and it was Sophie who cut the stupendous, double chocolate mocha cake. One of the children passed great-grandmother's hand-painted Meissen dessert plates. Nobody spoke. There was not much to say. You could hear the delicate clink of spoon in cup. A permissible scrape of fork on plate. They were eating the cake wondering, how is it going to be with Roberta gone?

Pauline's terrace was one more thing for her to admire. She called it one of her personal miracles. Furnished with light wicker like a living room, flower boxes along the broad balustrade, an avalanche of blossoms tumbling towards the blue tiled floor. Beyond the profusion of colors, the expanse of Mediterranean. Above, perennially azure sky.

Do I deserve all this beauty? It's my good fortune. It was my fairy godmother who, in her wisdom, gave me the brilliant idea to move here. I could have been sitting still — hovering, is more like it, in my old apartment back home. Day in — day out. Breaking the flow of hours with twice-daily trips to coffee houses. Around noon, with this one for coffee and cake. Around four in the afternoon, with that one for coffee and cake. Brrrrr .... Nice to meet one's friends and chat. But is it ever boring! Day after day. Brrrr .... She shivered again.

Time flies. Neck getting crêpy and crêpier. Like a turkey's. Hair mousier. Skin lumpier. Eyes sadder. What a life! Waiting for the inevitable to come and get you. Here, my neck is still crêpy — but how about this beautiful view? How about my bliss with Gogo?

She adjusted the large straw hat sheltering her cheeks.

How about feeling that I live a life of a novel's heroine? Gogo's said many times he does not mind my age. Mother in heaven, he's the age of my sons! I have to believe him. I must believe him!

She welcomed a light breeze on her naked arms, sat down facing the sea at the round table set for two. She delicately moved her slim body so as not to disturb the air.

Isn't my Yvonne another miracle? Would I have ever thought of having breakfast outside on Limoges china? She tucked her bare feet under the fluttering organdy tablecloth. And this fragrant, strong, black-as-night brew they call coffee here — it's all my Yvonne's doing. And she manages to be invisible. Does she know I'm in love? Where is my Jean-Luc?

And, as if called by a magic wand, there he was. Standing behind her. She did not need to turn to inhale his scent. Her Gogo. Felt his light kiss on the back of her neck. Inwardly she winced. Oh God, please let him not see the wrinkles. Please. Please.

With her hand moving nonchalantly through the lavender air, she invited him to sit.

"Bonjour, Jean-Luc. Perfectly on time. As always."

"Bonjour, ma belle Pola. Ma Belle Blonde."

That's what he called her now that her hair was tinted pale gold. She loved it. It suited her mood. He knew all those little things ... how to please .... He sat down. She touched his suntanned hand resting lightly on white nappery among frail cups and plates.

"It looks good, our *petit dejeuner*."

"Of course, it is wonderful, our *petit dejeuner*. Yvonne got *fraises des bois* in the market. Isn't the aroma overwhelming? The *brioches* came from the *boulangerie* you recommended. And coffee? — You know Yvonne, she is marvelous with coffee."

She looked into his brown eyes. He held her look. Smiled. They began to eat.

"The morning mail brought me a letter. Great news, Jean-Luc! My old friend I told you about, remember? Roberta. We called her Big Berta. She is coming. You never encountered such a generous person. She looks it, too. Compared to her, I'm willowy. Never mind. She's my oldest friend. You'll love her. We even attended some dancing lessons. You know, it's funny. Big as she is, she was always the best dancer. Apparently very easy to lead. Dance master said she floats. Isn't it strange? You'll see," she breathlessly added, "she's not like me. So organized. Orderly. And she cooks — divine!"

"Ah, non, non! You're in France! Here, wonderful ladies do not cook. Jean-Luc is going to explain this to your friend. Should we start looking for a dancing partner for her? I see you grimace, *ma Belle Blonde*. I understand. It's a NO. Guess we better wait till she comes. Roberta," he repeated, "Big Berta. One name too long, the other not appealing. We'd better think of a better name for her. How about, 'Bibi'?"

"Bibi, Bibi". She tried it on her tongue. "It sounds good. But, don't mention it at the beginning. First you meet her. She's going to stay with me until she finds an apartment. You'll see a lot of her. What do you think she's going to say when she sees you? She doesn't expect anything like this.... My big generous Berta will understand. One look at you and she'll know. We shall introduce her to Nice. She'll choose an apartment. I saw one advertised. The street above, what's it's name?" Pointed with her hand. "You know? Over there? It sounds good to me. Let her see it."

"Did you see it?"

"No. How could I? I'm too busy. It's all your fault. Bad boy. Either I'm tired, have to rest, or I'm with you. Or at the milliners. Don't forget the time at the milliner." Jokingly, she repeated, "Bad boy," patting his hand playfully.

"You remember what we're doing today? We have fittings for your shirts this afternoon. I'm sure they'll be perfect. With your body. Well, I'm not going to spoil you anymore. I'll not say a word. What would you like to do before that? I have shirting samples, we could go to Sulka, choose some ties? What do you think? Too early ? Oh, I forgot — the wine! You wanted me to speak to the wine merchant. I'll make a fool of myself. I know nothing about wines. I'll sound foolish. But you, well, is it possible to know more about wine than you do? I doubt it. I remember what you told me about your father teaching you. Aristocratic tastes. I do envy your background. So different from mine. I knew only about lumber and banking. That was my family's business. I told you."

"Nothing to envy, *ma Belle Blonde*. It's gone. Our very small vineyard sold. The chateau, if one could call it chateau, rented to some Americans. I don't like to think back. The wet, cold walls in winter, freezing bathroom I had to share with all my older brothers. Bah! I'm relieved it's done with. Well, true, wine I know. I'll speak with the merchant. You will only smile politely."

With admiration she watched Jean-Luc methodically choosing labels. Comparing. Tasting. Making arrangements with the wine merchant. What a guy! She loved the sound of his rapid French. She loved the little sips of wine tasting. She loved the whole process. "I'm tipsy!"

The bill was enormous, but so what? It was only money. Hers and for her to spend. Her sons could not possibly need more than they already had. Prosperous. Say it, Pauline. At least say it to yourself. Don't be shy. Here it's not *nouveau riche* to say "rich". They made it. Papa priming the pump, true, but nevertheless, they made it once more. It must be in the family. And here I am, lucky too. Careful, I might burst with all this happiness. Like the frog in the fairy tale ... so, down Pauline. Down girl.

"Jean-Luc, I think I'm a little bit tiddly," and giggled.

He, firmly holding her arm, "It's just as it should be. Wine is good for you, my Pola. You're in France."

"For all I know, you might be right. I feel so good .... Tell me, what was all that whispering after I signed the order? Eh? What was all that about?"

"Oh, nothing for you to worry about. Just making sure delivery'll be on time. One has to watch those people."

"Don't mind my asking, Jean-Luc, I love to know all you say and do."

He was carefully leading her by the elbow across the Croisette. "How about sitting down here," indicating the terrace of a small café, "for a demitasse? We could admire the sunset and discuss where we'll eat dinner."

Pauline was taken aback. "But I'll have to lie down a bit and change. Couldn't go to dinner the way I am now, could I?"

"Of course, *ma chouette*, of course not! And just for me, would you wear the pink frock tonight? The one I love? We could have a bite later, in the Casino. How about that?" with a knowing look on his expressive face.

"Oh, you rascal, you. Jean-Luc, you're something ... unbelievable. Yes."

Both Roberta and Pauline had happy tears in their eyes when they embraced. The larger woman enveloped Pauline in her arms. Berta's cases filled the small space in the hall, hardly leaving room to stand. One more kiss and one more. Pola beckoned her friend inside.

"Come in. Come in. But before you sit down, you'll have to admire my view. Here. My terrace. Is this something you ever expected? Is it?"

Outstretched arms embraced the fragrant air and the sky from east to west.

"Is it? Tell me, did I exaggerate?"

"No, you did not. Now I see. I can appreciate your enthusiasm. Every bit of it. Beautiful. Do you think I should rent something similar? How many bedrooms do you have?"

Pauline showed her two fingers. "Only two? It gives the impression of a larger place. And your maid, if she is a maid — she's cute. Any good?"

"You'll judge for yourself right away." Pauline called towards the door. "Yvonne, *ma chère*, will you unpack Madame Roberta's suitcases in the spare bedroom?"

"*Certainement, Madame.*"

Pauline added, "You'll see what a jewel she is. Oh, I'm so happy to have you here! Are you tired?" Gushing. "Today we'll eat at home. Yvonne will prepare for us a *blanquette de veau* and we shall break open a bottle of the best. To celebrate. But tomorrow, ha, ha, tomorrow will be something else. We'll go out. Do you know I eat out practically every evening?"

Energized with the presence of her visitor, Pauline bubbled on and on.

"We shall look at an apartment. Wow, am I tiring you? Do I talk too much? Go lie down for a bit. Rest. Do anything you want. Feel at home. I'll call you in an hour's time. Oh, I'm so happy ..."

"You're right, I need some rest." Roberta got up to kiss her friend. "It's nice to see you didn't change. Not a bit. Just the same as you were years ago. The same girlish, silly, bubbly girl. Only older. You know, we didn't even mention war! How glad I am. There is quite a bit of this talk going on. My sons-in-law, for instance. They say it's silly. There will be no war, we all know that. Hitler wouldn't dare! But talk — there is talk. I don't pay any attention to it myself. How lovely to have a respite from it! But here, in France, so far away behind the Alps, you are secure in any case. Even if something would happen."

"Same in Boston. In our Jewish circle they seemed to be worried about European Jewry. The future. But talking about this Hitler — well — there was talk. I think like your family, he wouldn't dare start a war."

Wine bottle almost empty. Yvonne went home. It was getting late and they still had so much to say to each other.

"So what did you do about Marysia?"

"Fanny took her over. She'll be so much better than the one she had."

"What a good idea. I was worried about that faithful soul. Perfect. She'll still feel part of the same family. What about our Luisa? How is she? Still so timid? While we're talking, I'm just thinking ... this," with a sweep of her arm encompassing all of the Riviera, " might be very beneficial for her. What do you think? Shouldn't we encourage her to join us?"

"Hold your horses. One step at a time. Let me settle, see about an apartment first. There is plenty of time."

"You're so wise. Always were. Let's wait till you settle. As you say, plenty of time. Berta dear, about tomorrow's breakfast." Slightly uncomfortable, slowly twirling the stem of the wine glass between her fingers. Chandelier's light blinking in the remnant of wine. "We'll eat on the terrace, of course, but I have to tell you something." Unsure how it would be received, continued, "I have a young friend who always joins me for coffee. You'll like him. He's very charming. I didn't want you to be surprised so early in the morning." Embarrassed by the attempted joke, she giggled and hurriedly added, "But sleep late. We're in Nice. There is no rush."

Berta's eyebrows rose a trifle. Eyes widened. She looked sharply at Pauline. So that was the catch! But said, "Don't worry, I shan't be embarrassed. I wasn't born yesterday. I sensed there must be something else behind all that happiness. But I won't give it a thought and I'll sleep like a baby. My motto, if it makes you happy — it's good for you. How old are you? I know, fifty-nine ... sixty — and I'm a year older. Let's stop counting."

"I knew you'd understand. I knew it! You know what, I told him so much about you, he thinks we should call you Bibi. What do you think about it? I'm telling you so that you can get accustomed to it. Bibi. It sounds nice, don't you think?"

Berta snorted. Burst out laughing. "Look at me. Do I look like a 'Bibi'? But then again .... Why not? In for a penny, in for a pound. I'll try to familiarize myself with it. What a nickname for a woman my age and my weight! Absolutely weird. Bibi. Bibi." she repeated at her door. And snorted again.

The sun was still in the eastern portion of the sky when they breakfasted. Roberta took in at a glance the young man clad in impeccable whites. Thirty, she guessed. Debonair. Well brought up. One could feel it immediately. But when she looked at her friend her heart sank. She shivered. My poor Pauline. In love. The stupid woman fell in love with a gigolo! Well. If it makes her happy, which it evidently does, why not? Why? She reasoned with herself, because it can't end well. That's why. And then, listening to the conversation, animated about nothing, why shouldn't it end well? I'm being gloomy. It does not go with the surroundings. With the banter of words. With the friendly glitter of Jean-Luc's signet ring in the sunlight when he lifts his coffee cup to his lips. Well, that's it then.

Plans were made for an afternoon stroll. For coffee at the Carlton Terrace in the late afternoon. For dinner at Bodega. To show Roberta the Côte's night life, they were to go dancing. To tango, fox-trot, before turning in. Nothing was mentioned yet about calling Berta "Bibi." To Jean-Luc, she was Madame Roberta. Way too early to be flippant.

In the nightclub, Jean-Luc spotted a friend of his at the bar. When taking a turn on the dance floor, he waved at him.

"Look, Madame Roberta, there is my friend, Philippe. I'll call him over. One more *Niçois* for you to talk to. He's fun — you'll see."

Pauline didn't know Philippe either.

"I thought I knew Jean-Luc's friends but he manages to surprise me at all times. So glad to meet you. How about joining us tomorrow for lunch?" Turning to Berta, "It would be fun, don't you agree?" Yes. She agreed.

The apartment Pauline had noticed advertised turned out to be, upon inspection, very satisfactory.

"Not as big as yours, Pauline, but it has this terrace here which goes around the bedroom. I like that. To get out first thing in the morning and be immediately in the sun. Ahm, yes. The awning. Good." She signed a lease, happy to be done. And out of Pola's way.

The very next day Yvonne presented her friend from a village near Grasse.

"My, Yvonne, that was quick! But you girls are so smart here, no wonder you know all that's happening. So your name is Pierrette? She says your ironing is perfect? Very well, let's see how we shall like each other."

The trio kept bumping into Philippe quite often. Wherever they went, he was there. Was it by design or accident? Joining them for dancing. Surely Jean-Luc's arrangement.

One evening, he pointed a well turned-out woman to Berta. "Chic. You see, Madame, this dress would suit you perfectly. I would choose for you a different color. Maybe pearl gray. Yes, I think pearl gray would be fine. You would feel good in it. The style is very Côte d'Azur."

She had to agree. It was a nice dress and the woman looked elegant. Well, when he suggested she make an appointment with the *Salon De Couture* and accompany her there — she looked at him thinking, aha. Now it comes. But here he was. Sunbronzed, handsome fellow. Age? She could guess it pretty accurately. About Jean-Luc's age. Am I being a fool? Or am I taken for a fool? I enjoy dancing with him. He smells pleasant. He continued talking, while Berta counted the pros and cons.

"I know fashion," he said. "I know fabrics. I'd love to help at the fittings with my ideas."

She looked sideways at him. And the way he pays my part of dinner bills is very discreet. I hand him the billfold, just like Pola does to Jean-Luc, under the table. Later he returns it to me when we're at my door. Nothing vulgar about the man. We talk cinema, food, fashion — the fellow has polish.

Her smile was followed by consent to the idea. "Yes, why not? Do go ahead, make an appointment with the *Salon*." Well, here I go with the flow.

Philippe chose the material. Measurements were minutely written down. A scarf added to the design against the evening's chill. It was decided she needed a different undergarment. Berta was musing, why don't they call it a corset? For goodness sake, I know it, they know it — it's a corset! Let's call a spade a spade. But mute, composed, she agreed to everything. Was quite pleased with the result.

Compliments from Pola and Jean-Luc encouraged her to remark,

"I thought Philippe's contribution very *apropos*. He knows about clothes and fashion. As a matter of fact I'm going to splurge, go back with him and order a whole new wardrobe. And hats. I need, so I'm told, a slew of new hats to match every outfit. I'm being completely 'worked over'. And you didn't hear the newest. Philippe thinks I should have a color wash for my hair. Did you ever? He thinks mine is too dull. Suggested bronze-red, to liven it up."

Alone, in private, Philippe put Roberta in front of a mirror. "Look at yourself. You are a full-bodied, well-built lady. Your skin is beautiful, your legs are shapely. Well, let's be bold about it. Let's make the best of it. Show it off. Add proper *maquillage* and you'll be looking as beautiful as you really are."

She smiled, looking at his serious face. He means it. He made himself believe it and he means it. Well, I'm lucky. The only thing for me to do is to believe in it too. And we're off to a new start. For me that is. Can I play the game? Let's see.

They were in a new, gay, *bôite-de-nuit* when a change to her name was suggested. Who started it? Berta missed the beginning. Anyway, "Roberta", according to the present company, was too serious, too long a name. "Berta" was not light enough, not "French" (meaning what? She did not get it). But then Jean-Luc came out with the "Bibi". That's nice. That's good. They immediately decided it was the right and proper name.

"From now on, you won't mind if we all call you 'Bibi', would you?"

Berta looked at their animated, laughing faces.

"It's silly, but all right! All right! You win!"

Pauline seemed particularly gratified. In the dim, soft light of the nightclub, her wrinkles vanished. She looked like a young woman. Pauline mused, how about me, how do I look?

"Pola, I cannot approve the nightly pantomime with the money. Changing hands. Changing billfolds. I find it demeaning. For me! I come from a business family — things are not arranged this way. Same with your family. How could you have stood it such a long time? I detest it. Bills are meant to be paid. Let's call a spade a spade. So, what do you think?"

"You're right, it has to be changed. I'll find other ways to put money into my Jean-Luc's pockets. But restaurants and so on — yes, let us figure out how much all that can come up to and give it to the boys — excuse me — men. I know you don't like me to refer to them as boys. They're men — let's give the men a sum in an envelope to spend on a monthly basis. Why do you make this funny face, Bibi?"

"Do you mean to tell me, Pola, you give Jean-Luc money like this, into his pocket? But I see, of course! It has to be done in some way. This seems to be the easiest way."

"Look, Bibi, the fellow has to pay for his lodgings, barber, etc... etc.... A million things. Doormen, for instance, and so on ..."

"Well, how I could have overlooked this angle is beyond me! I'll have to do likewise. And what I just said about coming from a business family doesn't add up! All this is simply too new to me. I make mistakes."

"Don't feel bad, my dear friend. You practically just arrived. You're new to the Riviera and you're learning." Embarrassed, she looked down at her freshly manicured nails and, in a voice as low as to be almost inaudible, said, "Berta, dear, I mean, Bibi, did Philippe take any liberties with you?"

"Philippe?" she snorted. "What an idea! Of course not! Look, dear girl. I know what's going on with you and Jean-Luc. You love him. You sleep with him. Me? It's different. I like Philippe. He is a good, pleasant escort. A good dancer, good company. I simply forgot about the economics of the transaction. How could I? I don't know. But I did. In answer to your question if he slipped into my bed, no! He did not. I don't know if he ever will. So that is that."

"Bibi, don't be mad at me, but I know he is very fond of you. I know it for sure." She lifted her eyes from her nails to face her friend. Don't be hard on yourself."

"What nonsense. I'm not being hard on myself. I simply do not seem to need IT. I'm fine. Oh, Pola, you're still the very same, silly girl you always were."

"Bibi, one more angle I want you to know about. So that you'll not be disappointed. I knew before, and now I've had it confirmed by my Yvonne. It's normal practice for escorts to take 'a cut'. A percentage, you know? When you buy, or order some stuff, you understand? I would not dream to think Jean-Luc would do differently. Would you? Those men have to look after themselves. Otherwise ..." she trailed off, miserable. "Oh, Bibi, say something, say it now!"

"My poor, poor Pola. Of course. I understand. I knew it from hearsay. Everybody knows it! Services rendered — services paid. Don't be so miserable. You and Jean-Luc have a different relationship. We all know it. I bet your Yvonne knows it. So come here, come to me Pauline, don't cry". Embraced warmly, kissed and patted, Pauline allowed herself to be comforted.

"Let's stop thinking about it. We both come from business families. We know full well how the world goes round."

That evening they danced again. Tango. Fox-trot. Asked even for some Charleston tunes. It was a grand evening. With a certain, special mood in the air. Later, they walked in the quiet night, breathing in the cool, blue moonlight. Went to another late night *bôite*. Danced some more.

"Oh, my feet. My poor feet." complained Bibi. "I lost weight. I really lost weight. I can see it from my clothes. Dancing every evening, no wonder! Can you see it? Yet I still seem to be too heavy for my feet. They do hurt me! My poor feet!"

Concern in Philippe's eyes. She noticed real concern in his blue eyes reflecting the candlelight glitter. Solicitous crease on his forehead. "Don't worry, Philippe. I can still walk. You'll not have to carry me home." And with the top of her hand she caressed his smooth cheek.

"I'll come in with you and give you a foot massage." he said, while holding her caressing hand firmly to his cheek. "You opened your eyes, Bibi, like you wouldn't know what a foot massage is? You don't? Well, one more reason for me to give you one. And I know how!"

In her bedroom, behind the silk-embroidered screen, she undressed and slipped on a robe. "Lie down here." he indicated the *chaise longue*, and I'll peel off your stockings."

"Oh, no, no. I won't go for that! That, I'll do myself. We've become good friends, but this is a no-no." She thought how glad she was that she adopted the custom of perfuming her body. And my feet do not perspire, thank God!

She stretched out her naked feet. He sat on the *chaise*, facing her. "Close your eyes, Bibi. In a minute you'll feel wonderful." He held her sore feet in both hands. Young, strong, sinewy thumbs started pulling, kneading her soles' muscles towards her big toe with a deep, measured stroke. Without releasing the sole, up went his thumbs with strength. Down lightly. Up again. Down again. First one foot. Then the other.

She closed her eyes. What a sensation! "I have to admit, Philippe, it feels very good."

"Wait, wait, I'll use some of your cold cream, it will be even better. Where is it? Ah, here — I see it."

Picked up her lightly cream-lathered foot and again started the strong, deep kneading pull towards her big toe. Later, she felt his fingers going around each small toe. Round and round. Coming back to the sole. My little toes are treated like babies, was her last thought, and she fell asleep. Her mouth relaxed. Lips opened a fraction letting out the most ladylike, delicate snores.

And Philippe, with an indulgent smile and Cheshire-cat movement, fetched the light, bed throw. Slowly covered her exposed limbs. The front door closed behind him without even the click of the lock to wake her up.

She was dismayed in the morning. Things are getting out of hand. How come I fell asleep? I'm walking too much. I'm getting too tired. We need a car. Now that Luisa is on her way to join us we definitely need a car. We have to go farther than the Casino in Monte Carlo and the Croisette. A large touring car. A Hispano-Suisa. That will do it. That's what we need.

"Philippe, allo? — allo? Is that you? I just wanted to tell you to come earlier. Yes, before lunch. We shall buy a car first and later join Pola and Jean-Luc for lunch. So, come over."

"*Enfin! Enfin, chère Bibi!* I was wondering when the idea of a car would occur to you. A Hispano-Suisa? It's a big one! Of course, your friend's arriving, we shall be five people! Ah, we'll all benefit from it. All of us. Do I drive? Do I know how to drive a car? What a question! Ask any full-blooded Frenchman on the Côte d'Azur! Everybody knows how to drive a car! It's good to be rich. To be rich ..." he trailed off longingly. Berta did not object to his remark other than saying, "Yes, it's good."

They met the others at the Salamander and after a leisurely meal, Philippe conducted them to a small *ruelle*.

"Aren't we going home for a siesta?"

"Yes, yes, but first," and with a grand gesture, opened the doors of the sumptuous limousine.

"Oh, Bibi, you kept it a secret!" Pola kissed and hugged her impulsively. "You didn't even say one word, and here it is! This beautiful car! Let's go to Menton, to Ventimiglia, to the Italian border!" Spreading herself on the white leather upholstered seat. "Jean-Luc, don't you simply love it?"

"You know where we should go? Beaulieu and Villefranche. It's very near. I just finished reading a story written by this fellow. Oh, what's his name? An American, so terribly popular. Scott something. Yes, I've got it. Fitzgerald, that's his name. Apparently, he has a whole *clique* of fans around himself and his wife. Funny name, his wife. Zelda. Is she Jewish? Zelda is a Jewish name, isn't it, Berta? Anyway, it says that those people sit around on the rocks all day long, smoke cigarettes in long holders and have a great deal of fun. We should check it out. Even if they stopped coming to this Villefranche, does it matter? There is a hotel — Hotel Welcome. A clown on a bicycle, one with an enormous wheel like in a circus — he rides around there. It sounds good. We could have dinner and see what's what. Who is with me? All right, shall we go?"

Before nightfall, Philippe drove Berta home. He got out of the car not only to open the door, but to kiss her hand.

"I know it's a custom in your country to kiss ladies' hands. We in France don't have that custom. Now I kiss your hand to ask forgiveness. I was rude. *Gauche.*" He looked deep into her eyes. "I mentioned money. I said it's good to be rich. It was a *faux-pas*. I wouldn't ever wish to offend you, not ever. I do care for you," and he kissed her hand once more. "I do."

Berta laughed. "I'm fond of you, too. And I forgive you. I'm rich, I know it. You know it. So let's keep proper decorum. All right, I'm four generations rich, did you know that? My great-grandfather started importing tea, spices and other goodies from the Far East. It stayed in the family. My children continue. They're fifth generation. The opposite of Jean-Luc's family. He is aristocracy without money. I have money but not aristocracy. But I know how to manage money. My father taught me. My husband taught me. I know. It's as it should be. I'm glad you apologized. With me it's forgiven and forgotten."

Luisa procrastinated as long as she could. With one cold bothering her after the other it was easy not to make a decision. In the end her apartment was emptied. Cases shipped and nobody left to say good-byes too. She realized how alone she had become. The last of her family. Inherited fortunes from parents who died before their time, from a brother lost in the war, from some rich, far-flung relatives in Berlin — all alone.

Why am I hesitant to leave Warsaw? The only thing I hear around here is about the war. Yes, war. No, war. There will be a war. There never will be a war. And I? I never know what I should do. I'm never sure. Am I doing the right thing now? If there is a war wouldn't I be better off well out of it — away from here — in France with my friends? They better be right, those two. Roberta has her head screwed on straight. But Pauline! She'll never grow up. Well, after all, they both seem to thrive on the Riviera. Maybe I'll at least get rid of my perennial colds? Oh, I wish to be happy. Others know how, why don't I?

Her two friends were ready to receive her. The small apartment in a *pension* they rented for her was full of flowers. Windows wide open, sun streaming in.

"We know how you don't like making decisions, so here it is — this apartment. You can give it up at any time. No lease. Not binding — so don't feel frightened. Wait a week or two. Stay on or give it up. As you wish."

When she met the young men, she did not need a diagram to realize what was what. For goodness sakes, she was sixty years old! Roberta, who, like the others, she now had to call Bibi, she did not fully understand. She always seemed so level-headed. Life is strange. She couldn't figure out how the change occurred in her. Pauline, well, Pola was always giddy. But they were all so nice to her! Showed her the sights. Didn't leave her alone even one day! She felt obliged to buy everybody a present. A blouse, a scarf, a bottle of perfume, even fancy toiletries for the two young men.

They were very attentive to her. Goodness, they even offered to introduce her to a dressmaker for proper frocks fitting this blessed climate. Yes — and her cold vanished! Gone. Overnight gone. It disappeared.

Jean-Luc suggested he'd introduce her to his cousin. Not exactly a proper cousin, he explained. There was something about a morganatic marriage committed in the last century. Goodness, life here was truly different!

Why Bibi and Pauline thought this such a good idea, she could not understand. She felt fine just with those two couples. And doesn't Pauline look different? Just like this actress, Pola Negri. Only the other has black hair and Pola is now a blonde. Berta had changed as well. The last time she saw her in Warsaw she was fuller, heavier. But of course, her new dresses, shoes, hats, all made a tremendous difference. Have to admit, she does look younger. And happy. And it's not even a year ...

Jean-Luc was in distress. He had a wonderful scheme in his mind. A scheme used before many times. Very successfully. Why not again now? But scruples ... scruples. They bothered his conscience. He liked Pola. She didn't bore him. Her girlish moods. Her outgoing nature. If you had asked him a few months back — he would not be as sure as he was now. She was fun. And her complete abandon in bed was a first in his career. The woman is full of love and sexual invention. It's a pleasure to go to bed with her. We are like a married couple. Not exactly a honeymoon, but then, hey, Jean-Luc, you'll never have a honeymoon! What do you know about honeymoons, you old warhorse!

The apartment he shared with two other young men (one a hairdresser, the other a bank clerk), was in mid-town Nice. It had two bedrooms. The daybed, they alternated. When Jean-Luc felt very 'flash' he bought off his old pal, the hairdresser, and the fellow took over his stint on the daybed. It was a nice apartment on a nice street. It had a telephone and a small, secure wall safe. That was the bank clerk's doing. "You never know," he said. "It's cheaper than a bank safe. We might need it."

Now Jean-Luc stood in front of this safe. Deliberating. His fist clenched at his mouth. Lips compressed. It was a big decision. After a moment, his fist fell to his side, mouth relaxed. The decision was made. He opened the safe and took out a small, black velvet jewelry box. Discreetly marked Van Clef & Arpels.

Autumn. The golden autumn of the Côte d'Azur. Before the rains start. It was still possible to have breakfast on her beloved terrace. But now Pola was bundled up in a warm robe and white cashmere shawl. As always her Jean-Luc appeared. Behind her, giving her her morning kiss on the neck. Just below the ear. She still shivered invisibly when that happened. This time, because of her shawl, she felt his light fingers where he had to pull away the soft wool to reach her skin. Double pleasure, she thought. I'm mad for him! I'm mad! But as before, as on all other days, she said, "Perfectly on time, Jean-Luc. As always." That's how mornings started ...

"Look Pola, look at this. Give me your opinion." And he opened the small square box, disclosing a pair of diamond cufflinks nestling on white satin.

"What do you think? A friend of a friend — you know how it is — has to sell. He desperately needs money. I have a little put away, money that is. If you were me, would you buy these? As an investment! He sells them cheap. Poor fellow, he really is in financial distress. What do you think? Should I splurge? Should I invest my savings in a couple of diamond cufflinks?"

Pola looked at him, freshly shaven, so handsome her Gogo. Her slim fingers delicately removed the glittering pieces. On her palm they looked even more impressive.

"You know, Jean-Luc, those will look very handsome on you. I think you should have them. Let's go this afternoon to Van Clef & Arpels and ask about their real worth. I have to go to the library. Bibi gave me her books to exchange and I have finished mine as well. So, it's not too far from the Avenue to the library. Let's go. I'll go myself. They probably will remember me. I was quite fussy ordering the monogram for your cigarette case. The letters inside the cover — you recall? — the words I wanted you to see and read when you pick out a cigarette? You didn't lose it, I hope."

"Of course not, *ma belle*. It's too showy for every day. As you see, I use this old thing here." He took a simple, silver case out of his jacket.

"How could I ever lose a gift from you? And such a costly gift to boot. *Ma Belle Blonde,* you are generous." And he cupped her small face between both his hands, bending over the empty coffee cups and remaining croissants to kiss her tenderly.

"Gogo, my Gogo," she said.

Late at night, when he let himself into his apartment quietly so as not to wake up the others — they were still up.

"What's going on? You're not in bed? That's unusual."

"Yes and No. We waited up for you."

Pointing at the bank clerk. "He saw you near Van Clef & Arpels with your elegant lady. We chilled a small bottle in case there was something to celebrate. Is there?"

Jean-Luc burst out laughing. "You fellows! You are impossible! I'm not saying! Not a word out of me!" but laughing, took a proffered glass of champagne. "*Salut!*"

In his pants' pocket, against his leg, he felt the small box with the cufflinks. In the breast pocket of his jacket, a thick packet of money in an envelope.

After his two buddies left for work next morning, Jean-Luc opened the wall safe. Took out his small safety box. Lock combination known only to himself. In it he replaced the little black velvet box with the diamond cufflinks and the packet of carefully recounted money. The sum of which now was added to a slip of paper he kept there as well. French to the core, he preferred to keep his fortune close to himself. Secure. Not in a bank.

With the change of weather they frequented the Casino. Now that picnics near Eze-en-Haut or Grasse were out, they sometimes had lunches at Bibi's or in popular taverns which they referred to as 'low life' and for the evening, a *'grand sortie'*. Ladies dressed to kill with sparkling jewelry. Men in tuxedos. Only little Luisa, who had a hard time to decide what sort of wardrobe she wanted to possess, only she looked like a little mousie. With her indescribable hair color, with her little nose and round blue eyes — she looked like a girl grown old prematurely.

They were becoming more and more like a family. Now, when bets became too large and luck was running out, Roberta had no compunction in wagging her index finger discreetly at Philippe. *Croupier* or no *croupier*, she didn't mind being seen. Philippe understood he was at his limit and turned away from the roulette table. The opposite was true of Pauline. It was Jean-Luc who knew the value of money. It was he who laid his strong, long-fingered hand on her pale, delicate one. His *Belle Blonde*. It was she who, like a good girl, got up from the gaming table to join the others for champagne and gossip.

And gossip there was galore. They pulled apart the other women in the casino. How coarse they looked. Probably German. Passing their table they overheard a few words in German, something about commercial possibilities. Of course! Black marketeers probably. Way too much adornment. To load oneself with diamonds! Who do they want to impress? Do they think they're Christmas trees? And the men accompanying them — a disgrace! Pola held on to Jean-Luc's arm.

"Look at that one! The one with the heavily pomaded hair. Goodness, he should be herding cattle to dress this way."

"His jacket is too tight, one can recognize bad tailoring at once. The other one, the blond fellow, I bet you the material is not Barathea."

"I would recognize it as such. Fool! I told you I know fabrics." from Philippe.

"Yes, you showed me at the *couturier* that you truly know fabrics. You did not explain how or why, so now, do — do tell!"

"Oh, you know, Bibi, one has or has not an artistic bent. I do. My mother recognized it, not my father. Not him. He was wrapped up in his drapery shop. He wanted me to join him in the future. But it was such a small shop.... Anyway, mother won and insisted on giving me piano lessons at least. I remember my piano teacher. You remind me of her, Bibi. Yes, you do. I loved her. She was also a large person. Like you, she had beautiful, well developed bosoms. Oh, did I ever dream of her bust! I dreamed I put my face between those two soft, white bulges. And of course, I woke up almost crying in frustration. But with my lessons it did not go too far. Money ran out. They had to stop. I was allowed to practice on the church piano, but lost interest. Still, one day, I'll show you how I can bang out some folklore tunes."

"Do, do play for us. You must! The taverna has a piano, didn't you notice? You must play for us one day." There the ladies insisted.

The group reached dessert stage at the Salamander when Maurice appeared. Jean-Luc stood up to introduce.

"Mon cousin". The dark-haired, middle-aged man went around the table, shaking everybody's hand.

"Would you join us for coffee," invited Pauline, who usually played hostess. "With pleasure." was the answer.

Jean-Luc indicated to the waiter with his raised napkin that one more chair was needed. A cognac glass materialized next to Maurice's coffee cup and conversation was picked up on the merit of one casino over the other.

Pauline, animated. Bibi, with unabashed, appraising eyes, scrutinizing the newcomer. Luisa, with sudden, deeply-pinked cheeks viewed the empty dessert plate in front of her with great interest.

I better look at him, she thought. Jean-Luc's recommendation. His cousin. The man who is supposed to become my escort. Goodness, do I need an escort? It's embarrassing. Still, I'll have to look him over sooner or later. What has to be, has to be. Slowly, so as not to make it apparent, sideways, she lifted her round chin. Fluttering lids over blue eyes. Slightly open mouth.

Just like a child prematurely grown and aged, Maurice noticed. He immediately appraised the situation. This is the rich widow, Luisa, the person he was supposed to become interested in. Well, it's going to be a new play with a new script. A bird, he thought. She's a small, gray sparrow.

Soon the group broke up. Hispano-Suisa deposited everybody at their own doorstep. Jean-Luc stayed with Pauline.

"How did you like Maurice?"

"Quite nice," she said, "but did you notice our Luisa? Poor thing. High time somebody became interested in her, or should I say showed interest in her? Jean-Luc, tell me the truth, is he going to take advantage of my friend? She's an innocent among innocents. And sentimental. Forty years a widow! Bah, did you notice how beet-red she became? With mouth half-open, she looked like an idiot ... poor thing, what is she thinking right now? Wouldn't be in her skin for a king's ransom. I'm so sorry for her. Hope she gets some fun out of life. With all the money she has ..."

"Don't fret, *ma Belle Blonde*," nuzzling her neck, "my cousin will manage to give her fun, maybe even to make her happy. He knows how." Started to hum *Auprès de ma blonde*, planting small, neat kisses on her ear.

"May I stay the night? I feel in such a mood." His hand on her breast. "Please, may I?"

Berta creamed her face thoroughly, searching for new wrinkles. Her *peignoir* slipped off her full, round shoulders. No, there were no new wrinkles. I should be satisfied. I am satisfied. All goes well. Actually, better than well. To imagine becoming like Pola. Infatuated. Crazy with love over a man. No, I can't imagine. She manages to find ways to touch him or his jacket even. It's like pawing him. Shame! Philippe is fun to be with. How many times I assured myself this to be true? But to lose my head — impossible! Have to buy him a present. That Pola, how she spoils Jean-Luc! Have to do the same. That gold chain. It might weigh half a pound. Geez. I'll get a similar one. Maybe with a monogram on the clasp? Could be *pavée* with tiny diamonds — not too expensive those — well, he'll be pleased.

If Pola asks me again if I sleep with him, I don't know what I'm going to do to that woman. The gall! It's none of her business. She needs it, I don't. That's that. But I love it when he delicately massages my back. He says my back is beautiful. What do I care about the compliments he pays me... I'm not stupid enough to believe him. But, it's very pleasant. I could use him right now. Now, about Luisa.

What are we going to do with Luisa? Will she be a hard nut to crack? Who knows, I might be pleasantly disappointed and she might soften quicker than I think possible. Now — when I'm looking at myself, looking, what do I see? A changed person. I did not look this way in Warsaw. I did not think such thoughts. To my family, I would now be unrecognizable. I remember telling them I might paint on the Riviera! Who has time to paint? I'm lucky to be able to squeeze some books into my busy schedule. Can't forget Luisa! The way she looked when Maurice came over! Her blue eyes when she eventually lifted them from her empty plate, so round and blinking, my god, what did Maurice think, observing her. Oh, I wish her well, our poor lost bird. And eventually she'll understand why we insisted she have an escort — exactly because we wish her well.

She left the *peignoir* where it slipped off her body. She now slept naked, luxuriating in the cool, smooth sheets she insisted having changed every night. Pierrette acknowledged the need for this — "*Madame est très chaude,*" she said.

Luisa closed the door behind her. Turned on the light. Looked in the mirror. What she saw in it made her squeeze her lips like a wronged little girl. Crumpled face of an old child about to start crying. She slumped on the *tabouret* in front of her vanity. Turned away from the mirror and got up slowly to turn off the light. Then she fell onto her bed, both arms around her head as though warding off heavy blows. She began a bout of quiet, heart-wrenching, crying and fell asleep with her face drenched in tears.

A knock on her door woke her the next morning. Flowers. An enormous bouquet of roses. Somebody sent her flowers. Her cheeks pinked. It must be this fellow, Maurice. He found out where I live! Does it mean I'm somebody? If he noticed me .... How nice. Oh, here is his card. What does he say? "Would you go out with me for a walk? I'm going to pass by this afternoon around four." Imagine! I didn't make the smallest encouraging move .... Of course, I'll go for a walk with him.

In a bit of a panic. What should I wear? The best would be my old stand-by, skirt and blouse. Which one? No, not this one, that one would be better. Hope it's good enough. I really must get some new clothes. Against the dressed-up ladies, I look like an orphan. Will ask Jean-Luc. He knows. Should I put on some rouge? Lipstick? My hair's so flat, can I fluff it up myself?

The "girls" phoned to ask her out for lunch. She excused herself with a headache. Oh dear, dear — do I need all that trouble? Luisa, Luisa — you do need this trouble, she admonished herself. You need to stand out, stupid. It's time you do something with yourself. Always the one standing in the corner ...

Had a hasty bite in the *pension*. Siesta time was a lost cause. She couldn't sleep a wink. At last, four o'clock. She was ready.

"Let's go up this street. There are small houses here, like the one I grew up in. I would like you to see it. My house is far away, near Toulon. But still standing. My sister lives there. I send her money to help out. She manages. Do you have brothers or sisters? No?"

And so they talked while walking and she duly admired the small, green-shuttered homes he showed her. Later, they had an aperitif for which Maurice ceremoniously paid. Although Luisa tried to pay at least her share he wouldn't allow it. The next morning a small bouquet arrived. Field flowers. She was touched because this one was more like her, demure, more suitable. And they met again. This time he allowed Luisa to pay.

Pauline was in stitches. What's happening? She sent Yvonne to the *pension* to spy out the "lay of the land", as she called it.

"Madame Roberta, myself, we both do not know a thing! Go, find out and come back quick. Don't dilly-dally. We're anxious."

Well, the news, when Yvonne brought it, was such that the two ladies congratulated themselves. "It's working! It's working!" Pola danced around the room. Ecstatic.

"Do you think they will become lovers?"

"Pauline, will you ever grow up? You have sex on your brain. That's not the issue. Lovers?" and she snorted. Rely on Berta to keep her head cool. "Who needs lovers? Not everybody. And anyway, it's none of your business." Inwardly she wished Luisa a better lot than to become infatuated with the man. Certainly not like Pola.

"Now for instruction, Luisa, listen. Tonight, you're joining us for dinner. You'll pass your billfold under the table. Like we used to do. Maurice is going to pay the share for you and himself. That's how it's done. Later, observe, see what we're doing. Do the same. You realize Maurice is not a rich man. To escort you will be his job. A gigolo. Make it easier on yourself, pay your dues. Hey, Hey! Don't cry!!"

But Luisa was already in tears. Slowly, inexorably, they flowed down her round cheeks from wide-open, blue eyes. With lips curved downward into a horseshoe she looked pitiful. Roberta had no patience with all this nonsense.

"Did you think he fell in love with you? You're sixty years old. Get a hold on yourself! Look at us. We do not cry. It's of no use to cry. He likes you. Be satisfied. He didn't need to make contact with you. But he did. The rest is just to make life pleasant and easy. That's how it's done. Do you understand? Stop slurping and get a grip on yourself. Brace up, girl. You're in for lots of fun."

Luisa looked from Berta to Pola. Searching for sympathy. And Pola did come through. Embraced her.

"Ssh — ssh — don't fret. It's going to be all right. Look at Bibi, doesn't she look happy? You will be, too. Look at me! Ssh — ssh — ssh — it's all right."

Well, it took a few short weeks and Luisa started to look different and to act bolder. Maurice was full of pride in the change.

"Look at Luisa. Look how lovely she looks in her new Chanel. Her hair bows suit her to a tee. Pastels are ideal for her coloring. They're talking about something called a permanent to curl hair — who knows what it is? I don't, do you? But soon she'll have it done to her hair."

Maurice himself assumed the look of a *boulevardier*. *Boutonnière* and all. It made him look older than his forties. Contrary to Luisa who, with *maquillage*, looked remarkably younger. What a change! Pola nudged Bibi.

"Look at those two. Do you believe it?"

"I see, I see. They're holding hands. Well, it's done."

The new 'couple' exchanged reminiscences. Maurice about his father, a garage mechanic at the time when cars were a great luxury and novelty. His infatuation with body-work, the accessories. Even with the motor works, showing his hands with pride, creases permanently black with cleaning grease. His mother making pocket money with village dressmaking. Slow going.

"Me, personally, I started helping in the garage, but didn't want to end up like my father. Decided to have a go in a city. Where money hides. Came here years ago and as you see, I'm still around." Luisa admired his pluckiness.

"Of course, I have a small dream. A small, but important dream. You want to know what it is? All right. I wish to own a car. What car? The best, the quickest, the sharpest machine! A Bugatti. A Bugatti sports car. And with luck, who knows? In time ... maybe ...." He was disarmingly frank.

"You know why I can speak to you so openly? Because being a widow of forty years has made you sensitive. Being alone has made you understand many things in life. I never encountered a less selfish person. When you look at me I feel you wish me well. Am I right?"

"Yes, Maurice, you're right. I wish you well. Tell me one thing. If I didn't have money, would you still like me?"

How can I be so bold? How, within weeks of meeting a man, could I have lost my sense of shame?

Openness invited openness. Maurice, holding her at arms' length, looked deep into her eyes. "I would love you."

In front of her door after dinner, when he embraced her, she knew it was a matter of time. Only a matter of time before she'd invite him in. Her bashfulness gone, she felt a great need to feel his body. All of his body. Naked body. "Go! Go!" she managed to say.

When did all this start? Was it with the daily flowers? Was that a message? And is that my response? He's worn me out with bouquets of flowers and when he turned away to go she laughed softly. He turned around.

"Why do you laugh?"

"Oh, a silly thought came to mind. Not important." She took the rosebud out of his *boutonnière*. "May I keep it?"

And when in bed in her demure nightgown, the rosebud pressed to her face, she fell asleep thinking, how is it going to be? Forty years have passed. Will I be any good? Almost wishing to have it over. Done with.

Pierrette, as thick as thieves with Yvonne. Those two knew absolutely everything that was going on around them. Visiting for short spurts with each other every day. Whispering when accompanying their two mistresses. Both on guard from the shopkeepers where their little cuts came from. Putting their francs away for rainy days. Like they were supposed to do. Soon they heard about the wife.

Yes, Monsieur Maurice had a wife. Near Toulon. Yes, a nice woman whom he kept tucked away. The little house was painted, repaired, kept in very good order. Everybody knew about the money coming in from Nice. Nobody talked. And Monsieur Maurice was too busy to visit. Obviously. It was understood. When asked, his wife assured her neighbors how well he was doing in the city. Kept her head high. Everything was as it should be.

Seasons were changing. Summers were spent mostly picnicking. Juan Les Pins beach was swamped with children and their nannies. Tourists were perched on the rocks of Nice and Cannes. The ladies commented. Congratulating themselves. "No war, see? We were right. After the first war, who needs another?"

Luisa, adjusted to her new status as a lady with a paid escort, actually found sex overrated. Now and then, all right, she didn't mind, but recognized the dilemma of Pola. The relaxed lifestyle of Bibi suited her temperament better. Maurice became her friend. She appreciated the value of this friendship. Each time he took her for a walk in the city, somehow they ended up in front of the car dealer's. Look at this little Bugatti! She looked.

And one day bought it. A red, cute, neat sports car. Maurice found it on his birthday in front of Luisa's *pension*. Delivered the very same morning. He saw it immediately. He knew it was for him. His eyes watered. The little handful of daisies fell out of his lax fingers.

Luisa waited for his arrival at one of her windows. How wonderful, she thought, to be able to make somebody so happy. She ran out to greet him and saw his tearful eyes. Speechless, he turned from the car to her, from her, back to the car, and back again to her. She stood near him and enjoyed his happiness. With only a smile and a little flutter of heart. Not a word was exchanged. Then he opened the car door for her to sit down on the red leather seat.

Jean-Luc discussed the Windsors' wedding with Pauline. The Duke's abdication created quite a stir among them. The world news was not exactly followed in their circle. Newspapers not even scanned. But this was a great, big DO. Almost in their backyard. The Duke and Duchess, photographed in all magazines. Her dress and hat for the ceremony — all important sources for gossip and appraisal. And the absence of the Royal Family. Well, this was quite an event.

Jean-Luc played with her slim hands. Almost absent minded. He pulled off her diamond wedding ring and kept putting it back on again. Off and on.

"I assure you, Pola, I know, the Duke is friendly with this awful Hitler. She, as well. They both are. Believe me."

Pola listened to him, but kept her eyes on the ring. On and off her finger. At a certain point she took it out of his fingers and gently put it on his pinkie.

"Here. Keep it."

"Pola, no, no! I don't want it." And she, "Yes, you do. You do want it. And I'm giving it to you. I like doing it. So, there ..."

He kissed her naked finger, her hands. He pulled her close to himself. And like always, always, after getting something costly or personal, they ended up in bed. She knew it was coming. She did not mind it. Definitely didn't get angry. This was a habit. Established. Honored by custom. This was part and parcel of having Jean-Luc for a lover.

"I have other rings."

Good movies in cinemas. They liked comedies. Laughed uproariously. The six of them were a closely-knit group. There was no way to keep a secret between them. The outside world was completely shut out. Bibi answered Pola's question of, "Why don't we fight with each other? Tell me why?"

"We were friends before we came to the Côte d'Azur. We knew each other from time when! Look around, it's in most cases the females who fight over the young man, compare, have crises. Men want peace and loot. Lots of loot. As much money as they can get out of us — don't fool yourself ..."

"I don't, Bibi. I know it. Don't rub it in! Still I do know Jean-Luc loves me. In his own way, but he does. Nothing you say can change what I know to be the truth. He loves me."

"Pola, dear Pola, it's too late for us to have a fight over this. I admit — I'm wrong — you're right." And so, again peace reigned.

A long letter arrived from the States. Pauline read it — her face pale, incredulous. They must be crazy. What are they talking about? Let Bibi have a look at it. It was a letter from Pola's sons. In short, advising her that informed circles in the U.S.A. were sure a war was imminent. Only a question of time. When. Get ready to move out and to come to the States. Berta shook her head.

"You know, it makes sense what they say here. It sure makes sense."

Pola banged her fist on the small table.

"They're crazy, crazy, crazy. They don't know what they are writing about. We have here Les Alpes Maritimes. What war? They're mad! How could anyone come over here? We're secluded from the rest of France."

Bibi admitted, "You might be right. Who knows? I prefer to think like you. There will be no war! End! As a matter of fact, France has the Maginot Line. That is a powerful barrier. Better even than the mountains."

The matter rested for weeks. Then a letter came from Poland. Very significant. Roberta's daughters wrote at length, while her sons-in-law scribbled confirmatory postscripts. In short, "Come home! There might be a war. You're better off with the rest of us here in Warsaw."

One could not ignore it. The only one without pressure to go somewhere was Luisa who, being alone in the world, could not have anyone warn her about an 'imaginary' catastrophe. But even she was not immune to influences. The atmosphere changed. The three women were irritable, unsure. The young men subdued, very attentive and consoling in word, gesture and deed. Jean-Luc mentioned the need to get in touch with his family. Philippe cautiously spoke of a possibility to go up north. Maurice thought about Toulon...

The atmosphere soured. It was not the same anymore. Then in quick succession night telegrams started to arrive for Pauline. More than twenty-five words each. The last one threatening. Do pack up, liquidate, or else. The "or else" referred to a codicil in her late husband's testament allowing the sons, who were her guardians, to stop the flow of money. Disaster!

Pauline was in hysterics. Nobody could stop the flow of tears, the wild flailing of arms, the prostrate body, weeping, curled up on her bed. Her eyes red, face puffed up. She, in her pain, could not even stand the touch of her beloved. Pushed him away. His embrace only emphasizing what she might miss in the future. Looking through tears at his dear head, she saw him lost to herself. Forever. It was not to be borne. She collapsed in a heap. Jean-Luc did not leave her bedside. She was sick — sick with love lost before it was lost. Then a brilliant idea occurred to him.

"*Ma Belle*," he said, "listen to me, stop for a moment, listen to me. You can send for me — I'll come to you the moment I get the papers — the necessary visa — I'll come. Will this please you? Because I swear I'll come."

That was a little better. Now her tears were more manageable. And she started to pack. There was no way she could stay in Nice without any money. She opened her jewelry box and took the valuable trinkets, her diamond bracelet, other rings, a brooch or two.

"Take it, Jean-Luc, keep it, *mon amour*." And he did, adding it to his safety cachet.

The day soon arrived when her cases were picked up. With a swollen, but well *maquillaged* face, she turned away from the whole group. Her fingers still trailing on the sleeve of Jean-Luc's jacket. Eyes bravely looking ahead, without turning her face, she boarded the train to Marseilles.

Roberta was quietly liquidating as well. There was no way she could ignore the wish of her whole family to be together in case ... in case there might be a war. Times were very precarious — and she admitted they were in their right to have her at their side in case a war really did break out. How could she give them an additional worry about herself far away in such a case? Not only far away but divided by two frontiers. The nebulous possibility of an outbreak of war became more of a reality. Two frontiers. Difficulty in communication. They were right. She was going home. Philippe was distracted.

"I'm going to miss you," he repeated every day.

And he came each day while she was packing. They revisited their old haunts. Spoke to the waiters. Took their good-byes. A sentimental journey. Drank alot of champagne. "I'm going to miss you." And ordered one more bottle. Bibi was drunk. Night after night. Not tipsy, but drunk. Firmly closed her door for the night. Not for her, last minute sex with Philippe. She was leaving a way of life. He, being only an integral part, not the physical center of it.

What was the physical center of her life in Nice? Nothing. Nothing but freedom. Freedom from family, censure, memories. Even from worry. Complete freedom to do as she felt when she felt like it. Benevolent lifestyle in a benevolent climate. That's what she was going to leave behind. Her last gesture the day of departure was the Hispano-Suisa. The keys to the car. Without any ceremony, casually she handed them, dangling from a finger, to Philippe.

"Here. My last present to you. Have fun."

She left with a gigantic headache. Well, of course, he took her to the station. He opened the door to her carriage in the *Wagon Lits*. He handed her the latest Vogue, Harpers, Life, through the lowered window of the first class compartment. Two tears coursing slowly down his handsome, deeply tanned face. But his Bibi touched her aching head and frankly looked towards the imminent possibility of closing her eyes and maybe asking the *Wagon Lits'* attendant to give her a cold compress to put on her forehead.

"Philippe, forgive me, but I have a monumental headache, can't see straight. We drank too much champagne ... I have to lie down. Forgive me ..." The whistle blew. His hand waved good-bye at the empty window. The *Train Bleu* was off.

Arrived in Warsaw's Central Station on the last day of August. Her family waiting with troubled faces. Roberta, in contrast, looking young, even fresh after the long journey.

She found the city tense despite the bright fall colours. Chestnut trees as beautiful as the days she had left. It was warm, balmy even. But the air was permeated with the chill of impending doom. And rightly so, because on the next day, September 1st, German airplanes flew above Warsaw.

From then on they all got sucked under, disbelieving. Almost watching themselves swallowed inexorably by events. Within a few months Roberta vanished, as did her entire family. Beyond anyone's imaginings all vanished to appear only later, much later, on a list of those gone.

Luisa was the only one of the three left. For her there was no other place to go. Maurice mentioned Toulon a few times but somehow was still at her side. She felt forlorn, sad, bereaved. They were visiting all the places visited with the others. Sometimes they met Jean-Luc. Sometimes Philippe. In time they stopped using the Bugatti, which stood cleaned, waxed, and polished in Maurice's friend's garage, covered with a heavy tarpaulin. It was his and he was saving it. Tourists left.

Replacing them, thousands of French refugees from the north filled every room in every apartment. Hotels were jammed with those who had money. Everywhere new faces. Worried faces. Nice wasn't like Nice anymore. Nor Cannes like Cannes. One morning a note was handed to Luisa. From Maurice. She knew what she would read in it. How funny. We started with a note and we end with a note.

Yes, of course, he left to join his 'sister' in the village near Toulon. She didn't know its name or where it actually was located. But so what. Somehow it stopped being so important. Nothing was important. Life was just one day to be lived after the other.

In the cafés where she was well known from days gone by, she heard that Jean-Luc, (the Patron called him *"Monsieur le Baron"*) joined the *Maquis*. Somebody else told her that Philippe was taken prisoner. She herself shed her acquired elegance, her Chanel suits and hair bows. She became a little gray sparrow again. Known only to those who knew her from the bygone days. The others thought her to be slightly off her rocker. Because, frankly, sometimes she talked to herself. Those who knew her, did not mind. The others, she did not mind.

And *la Belle Blonde,* Pauline? Poor thing. Before she could try to bring over her Jean-Luc, before she could even find out where he was — after the hurricane of war subsided. Five years. Five long years. Before that, she went herself. Her sons said, "We gave her all possible comforts. She was an aged lady. It was her time." But no. No, that was not the case. Or the reason. She willed herself to die. Could take just so much loneliness from her love and not more. And so old, so old, she felt so old. Just gave up.

Luisa was haunting Nice. Her rheumy eyes recognized places she considered part of her real home. Quite often not allowed to pay for her drinks, or meals. For old times' sake. The old timers looked after her. The old timers even knew where she lived. The same old pension. Only now she occupied one room at the back. No, she was not destitute. She had enough money. She only looked that way. Destitute. Mumbling to herself. Going from café to restaurant to *boîte.* Mumbling. Looking down at the pavement at her feet. One step after the other. Alone.

LILA

Lila was bored. Bored with her bed. Bored with the four walls of her room. Bored with the chain of housekeepers, nurses, with the food she was given. Bored with her life. How tedious to wait for her son's infrequent telephone calls. For her daughter-in-law's weekly visits. Grandchildren did not drop in anymore. That's sensible. If I were Max or Joanie I would never call on a bedridden, silly old grandmother like me. If they would just leave me alone. Let me sleep.

A little thought crept into her mind. It made her smile. Involuntarily. She could not rid herself of this smile. She almost giggled. Through half-closed lids she saw herself alone in the room. Good. It would not do for them to see her smile. Oh, but it was fun! The couple who stayed with her — such bores — the woman patronising (stupid cow). I aimed well (the slipper was too soft). Still, it hit her fat ass. Ha, she did not expect me to move so quick, she and her precious husband. The second slipper almost hit her head — I aimed well — it was fun. And now they are gone, thank God — and good riddance.

But then, from her daughter-in-law, Mandie, "Mother, how could you? Those were good people! I have to call the agency again. Who knows who they will send over this time?"

Lila wanted to say: I don't care. What's the use of saying it? Nothing will change — only this is left — bore, bore, bore. Instead she said, "I'm sorry." Turned her face to the wall, eyes closed.

The phone was dialed. She listened attentively to what was said to the agency.

"My mother — you remember? She is an invalid. No, not too sick, it's more nerves than real sickness. I must have somebody right away, I have a dinner party tonight, have to be out of here soon. Yes, very dependable. She will have to keep house here as well. You have it all in your file. Right away. No, money is no object, but you see, she cannot be left alone ..."

Lila had heard it all before. Many times. She dozed off.

Later when she opened her eyes this person was here. In her room. This stupid cow is thin, Lila thought. I don't even like her face — a sourpuss — but oh! how she smiles at me! She calls me "dearie"! How dare she? Back home I would have kicked her out right away. Here, yes, here, she will have to stay. What is she saying? Let her talk, I will not listen, I will not answer — talk — talk — talk. . .

For some days there was peace. Her son, Joe, kept his fingers crossed. Mandie expected the dreaded telephone call any day, any hour. Tried to relax on Valium. Each passing day like a gift. She even sat with the children around the swimming pool. In the blessed sun. Slept through the night. Almost.

And then it came. The phone call.

"I'm packing. I'm leaving. Right away. Will not stay around this loony one more hour. You know what she did? She pushed the whole bowl of porridge into my face. I cannot get it out of my hair! She is crazy, your mother. She should be behind bars! You take care of her!"

And that was that.

"I have to tell you, Mother, you drive me crazy. What am I to do with you? I cannot stay here with you. You cannot stay with us. The children and their friends all day long in and out of the house. It's not for you. You know it. We discussed it years ago. Remember? Together with you. We decided the best way for you is to live in your own house. Nobody can bring back your husband but with proper help you could be satisfied, even happy here. Why are you giving us all this trouble? Why can't you live with your help in peace? You know you abuse them! What was wrong with this woman who just left? You don't want to talk about it? All right — O. K. — but for God's sake, what am I going to say to the agency?"

Before turning her head to the wall Lila murmured, "I'm sorry." What else was there to say?

From the living room Mandie's voice floated in.

"I know this situation is preposterous. But again I have to get somebody right away. Now! What are you telling me? You've run out of housekeepers? How about a nurse? True, she would have to keep house. There would be practically no nursing. Yes, I see, they refuse. So what can you do for me? A man? You must be joking! What would people say?"

Lila pricked up her ears. That sounded different. Who would that be? A yokel — a male idiot for a change? By craning her neck Lila could glimpse Mandie at the phone. A frowning face. Concentrating while listening to the other side. "I see ... I see ... " After a prolonged pause she said,

"This I cannot decide by myself. This is for her son to decide. Let me tell him all you just told me and I'll get back to you right away."

That's how Boris, for the past 25 years an orderly in the General Hospital, just recently retired, came into Lila's world. A short, stocky man, built rather like a bear with a scraggly peasant face.

"Mother, this is Boris. He was born in Russia. He will take good care of you. He knows how, I was assured. But do not be alarmed, it will not be for long. You do speak Russian, I remember you telling me. Anyway, he speaks English well. And the agency promised me to try hard to get a lady for you like always. So it probably will be only for a short while."

She took Boris away to show him his room, the layout of the apartment and to give him the weekly housekeeping money.

Later, when he came back alone to her room, he smiled. He smiled nicely. A shy smile. Large, spaced teeth. Lila liked that. Liked his eyes. Brown, honest eyes. She made sure nothing of this showed in her face. Did not say a word. His voice deep, chesty.

"I cannot call you Madame Golden. Will you permit me" — this almost shyly — "to call you Miss Lila?"

She barely nodded with her chin. At least he shows respect.

"What would you like for supper? I know how to cook. Nothing fancy, but I could find something in the fridge to surprise you. Would you like that?"

She nodded again with her chin. When was the last time she was asked what she would like to eat? When was that? She could not remember. Something stirred pleasantly in her mind. For sure this here Boris was no idiot.

She liked the paprikash. Like in the olden days. She liked it alot. How she was tired of chicken. Always chicken. This was red with paprika, fragrant with bay leaves; it tasted peppery, salty, it even had *nockerln*. Now she said her first words to Boris: "Where did you learn to cook like this?"

"Oh, that was in Europe. Long ago. I worked for a while in a restaurant, but I was trained as an army orderly. One day I will tell you. It's a long story. Now I better brush your hair. It needs brushing. And I will get you ready for the night."

He did brush her hair. Carefully, delicately, undoing the tangles without pulling.

"Have to tie it up with ribbons. Where are your ribbons?" Lila did not have any. "No? Then tomorrow I will get you some. Red should suit you. When I go for groceries I will buy them."

Lila woke up next morning full of anticipation. At first she did not realize why this little flutter inside her, why this excitement — then she remembered, aha — Boris! Let's see how this day will go. It started very well. Her cream of wheat had a sprinkle of brown sugar and cinnamon with a dollop of melting butter in the centre. And coffee. This was real coffee. Full of aroma, strong, like coffee was meant to be.

She smelled a whiff of freshness when Boris bustled in and out of the room. She knew it meant the other rooms were being aired. And when he put his head in to say, "I'm off to the grocery store," she decided to say thank you, later on his return. But she forgot. She forgot because Boris kept her so busy. "Where is a small mirror?" She had to think and then point to it. He needed a comb.

"It must be in that drawer," she said.

Gray hair neatly parted in the middle and braided into sparse pigtails.

"Miss Lila, do you want single bows or double bows?"

She wanted double bows and extended both hands to hold up the mirror to her face. And quickly dropped it.

"It looks silly," she said.

"Why, Miss Lila, how can you say such a thing! You don't look silly, you look pretty, but a little pale — where do you keep your make-up?"

Lila did not remember. "It's so many years. I forget. Before the funeral. Long before the funeral." She became impatient. "No. No. I don't want make-up. Don't you know? I'm sick!"

"Miss Lila, I don't want you to talk like that. You are going to get better. You will see. Soon. I promise and when Boris promises... I bet I'll find your make-up — it should be in this drawer. See? I found it. What we want is a bit of rouge. Just a little here and a little there."

Reluctant, holding herself back stiffly, she let him apply rouge to both cheeks.

"Now look in the mirror, Miss Lila. See how nice?" He dropped the mirror in her lap. "I'll make you a surprise lunch." Lila protested mildly — "But I have a diet."

"I know your diet. I keep it. Remember yesterday's paprikash? That was chicken. Ha! — you did not recognize. I like cooking. I often cook for the couple who share my flat — now — I'll cook nice for you. You'll see." Lila fiddled with the small mirror, then raised it to look at her face. Quickly dropped it. "I look stupid." Boris turned the radio on without comment.

Lila was not quite sure. Did she look stupid?

What woke her from her afternoon nap was Boris. Rummaging in the cupboard. "What are you looking for?"

"Are you up? Good. It's not right to sleep too much. I'm looking for something pretty." He held up a small pile of bed jackets. "Let me put this one on you. The pink one. Oh, now you look a proper *Barinia*. That's nice, a real lady."

Lila fussed with the frills, quite pleased.

"A cup of tea. Now is the proper time for some tea." He brewed a strong cup of tea. "Do you know how to play dominoes?" And after dinner he sang to her. A sad Russian *dumka*. "You know it?" She nodded, yes. Boris said, "Next time we sing together."

The day was utterly exhausting for Lila. What did he say? He called me a *Barinia*. With this she fell asleep.

Mandie willed herself not to phone, not to inquire how Lila was getting on with Boris. Better let sleeping dogs lie. If there is a catastrophe I will hear about it soon enough. I shall go over there when I'm supposed to, Thursday afternoon, when this Boris fellow will take his two hours off, she mused. What if this arrangement could hold? No, it's impossible.

Joe asked her every day, " Did you call the agency? Did you hear from the agency?"

"Yes, Yes, I called. There is nobody better available. But they promised, you know they promised the moment a candidate registers, immediately..."

In the meantime, Lila was giggling. Boris changed the way he was doing her braids. Twice he changed it. Each time she had to watch him do it. And he washed her hair. Now she felt embarrassed when he sponged her. Her mind going furiously over and over a new idea. Maybe, maybe she could have a bath? One day he brought a bottle of nail varnish. Now she had painted nails. She giggled alot. When Thursday came Lila sat straight up in her chair, propped up with pillows, her fingernails in full view, waiting for Mandie's visit. And when she came Mandie just stood there. In the doorway. Mute, at first.

"Mother, your cheeks are rouged!"

"Yes," Lila said and twittered, "and my nails, look at them!"

145

To Mandie she was hardly recognizable. In the fresh, pretty bed jacket, rouged, smiling and those silly braids. Her cheeks looked filled up — had she gained weight? It's barely a few days. I'll just cross my fingers again. How is such a change possible? Joe. Joe must see how she looks. He will not believe me when I tell him. If it could only last...

Joe came the same evening. As Mandie said, here she was, his bedridden mother in an easy chair, looking so well and smiling at him. Remarkable.

Boris was brushing her hair for the night, proudly announcing: "After I finish this, Mr. Golden, I will massage your mother's neck. It's good for her." Lila nodded. "Yes," she said. "we are going to walk soon, Mr. Golden — yes, Miss Lila and I — we shall walk."

And Lila looked up at her son. Nodded. "Yes," she said.

Later, at home, he discussed Boris with Mandie. At length. Should they let the agency know or not? Was it too early? Mandie was for telling them right away: stop looking for a replacement. It seemed to her that in time Lila would get even better. But Joe was unsure. He had misgivings.

"I don't know, Mandie. It's too good. It's too quick .... Let's see, Let's wait."

Boris devised a whole routine for massages. Feet and legs. "To make you walk, Miss Lila. You will feel tingling under your skin, it will be your blood flowing faster. Just wait." He was right. Because soon after she was able to stand up. With a cane and his arm at the ready she did walk. Slowly, but she did.

Now, finally, Lila could tell of the plan she devised for a bath. A proper bath. In her proper bathroom. This sponging had to stop. She was blushing. Small hand towel covering her breasts, her private parts, and Boris chattering, chat chat chat — she, not even listening.

"Miss Lila, for me this is my job — do not pay attention to what I'm doing. I washed hundreds of people. Of course you are special and you are prettier, but washing is washing, one — two — three — and it's over — you see?" And so it was, over.

The twice-weekly rite started with a walk to the bathroom. With a big sheet. With a bathrobe. With a kitchen stool. With Boris keeping his eyes closed. With Lila's twittering. With Boris averting his head while she slowly swung her legs over the rim of the tub and into the shallow water. Warm and scented with green, pine bath salts. She stretched. Closed eyes. Luxuriating.

Too exhausted to walk back to her bedroom, he had to half carry her.

Now it was winter. Boris fiddled with the fireplace. It draws well. I will phone your son, Miss Lila.

"Mr. Golden, here is Boris speaking. You recognize my voice? Yes, my accent. I want your pemission to settle your mother, her bed and her special chair in the living room. There is this fireplace. I checked it. It works well. Why shouldn't your mother enjoy it? I am a careful man, nothing can happen. It will be just fine. Oh, thank you. I'm happy for Miss Lila. And one more thing, Mr. Golden. Your mother sometimes sings with me, you know, those old Russian songs she knows. If I could have your permission to bring my balalaika? Yes, thank you very much. It will make your mother happy."

And she was. She looked up at Boris with limpid eyes. She smiled sweetly at him. She was shy one minute, flirtatious the next. Boris going about his tasks humming. Full of energy, purpose and vitality. Sometimes calling her "my Princess." Fussing every day with the fireplace. Tapping the bricks.

"What do you want with those bricks?"

"Have to make sure all is well, Miss Lila."

She was glowing. Proverbial winter winds were howling outside. Blowing snow piled high on the old lilac branches while they were playing their secret little games and jokes.

Mandie and Joe came back from Florida. Tanned and refreshed.

"Your mother has come alive, did you notice, Joe? She is not the same person. It's truly amazing. And the apartment, did you notice, Joe? How clean it is? Like never before. Wherever he came from, this Boris had very good training. I think we should show our appreciation. You know, he should be getting a raise and who knows, maybe a bonus for Christmas as well. What do you think?" Joe agreed. Reluctantly, "What's the matter with you? Don't you see? Think back a while. Did you ever expect such a change?"

"Alright, Mandie. I did not. But I agreed about the money, did I not? What more do you want from me?"

"Oh, nothing! As long as you agree. Only I don't understand your attitude. I can see something is bothering you." But here the matter rested.

Boris was effusive in his thanks. Lila? Lila did not know about monetary transactions. It was Joe. Her good son, Joe, who always managed her fortune. From the day her husband departed, he took over. As generous and understanding as his father before him.

By now Lila was walking about the apartment with a cane. Touching a *bibelot* here, a doily there.

"Miss Lila, do you know Spring will be here soon? This old lilac tree in your garden, soon it will be full of purple flowers. Do you like lilacs, Princess?"

"Oh, Boris, you know I love lilacs, I love all flowers. Now that I can walk so well we shall go down to the garden — there is a little bench under the tree ..."

Boris pampered her with back rubs. His big strong hands felt velvety on her frail back. She could have laid on her bed for hours on end while he was massaging her. Up and down. With long, muscular strokes along the delicate spine. Sometimes singing. Sometimes telling stories of his Ukraine while pressing her flesh. Here and there he gave her a tickle. As a matter of fact, he tickled her quite a lot. He said, "I like when you laugh, Miss Lila." And sometimes when the fire glowed with warmth and colour, sometimes, not often mind you, but sometimes, he quickly bent down and kissed her on the shoulder. Just like that. After which she slept like an angel.

Mandie and Joe were returning from the theatre. Passing their Mother's quiet street, Joe said: "It's only ten o'clock. Let's see what those two old birds are doing. Look, the lights are on in the hall and in his room. Sort of darkish in Mother's room — let's drop in on her."

"Oh, Joe, how silly you are, but you *are* the son. You want to kiss your mother goodnight, why not? It will make the old girl happy, I'm sure."

He parked the car, found the front door key on his key chain and opened the door to a distinct sound of laughter. Lila's and Boris's laughter. He looked at Mandie. Mandie looked at him.

"What's going on? For God's sake, it's ten o'clock at night! What is there to laugh about like that at this time of night?"

Quietly they sneaked upstairs. Transfixed, they stood at the door just at the very moment when Boris finished a tickle, bent down and kissed Lila's exposed shoulder.

It was not Joe. It could not have been Joe. It was a wild beast roaring. He stood on the threshold, terrible noises emanating from his very insides. Poised for a jump at Boris's back. Would have leaped and struck him if it were not for Mandie's restraining hands. Holding him back.

"No, No, No, Joe, No."

His jacket pulled awry, face contorted with impotent fury, he swore, "You bastard — you pervert — I'll kill you — I'll put you away for life!"

He kicked a chair. It turned over. He kicked the fireplace. A loose brick slipped out. Like a flash he pulled it out to lash out with it when something stopped him. Behind the brick. There! He stooped and pulled out — what is this? Money. Plenty of money. Dollar bills spilled from his fingers to the carpet, like leaves.

"You stole! Mother! Mother! Look, he is a thief! He stole money from you! On top of everything else he is a thief."

Boris facing him, mutely, arms in rolled up shirt sleeves helplessly hanging at his sides.

Lila sat up. Eyes round with fear. Holding a sheet's corner to her chest. Pale as a corpse in the rosy light from the fireplace. Mouth half open to shriek. And she shrieked. And shrieked and shrieked. Like a wounded animal. Walls of the room closing in on her. Ceiling pressing down on her skull. Between her ears, ocean pounding. Dark and ominous. Air — air — there was no air to breathe — she gagged — cold black waves closed over her head. Overwhelmed, she fell back.

"Joe, stop! What did you do? Look what you did! Dear God! She fainted! Do something! Somebody! Boris, do something!"

Joe collapsed. Slumped on the sofa while Boris ministered to his mother. Held his head with both hands, elbows resting on knees, weaving from side to side in utter despair. Mandie near him. Stroked his back. "It's not your fault," she whispered. Looked at Boris. "Can I help you, Boris?" Mutely, he shook his head. Lila seemed to have come out of her swoon. Lying quietly on her side, turned towards the wall, with eyes closed. In fetal position, small and frail under the white sheet.

It was decided that Boris would be packed, ready to leave the moment a replacement arrived in the morning. Now in the middle of the night, nothing could be done. Joe wanted to stay in Mother's room till daylight but Mandie firmly opposed. "You come home with me. Nothing can happen here. Mother seems to be asleep. Boris will be in his room with the door open and you, you must have a proper rest in your own bed."

Without a word spoken all understood that whatever happened here, this event would remain secret. The family could not afford to have it come out. That was obvious.

When Boris was sure they had left, he slipped out of his room. Bending over the inert body of Lila, whispered,

"*Dzievochka*, Princess, it was not for me, this money. You must believe me. It was for you. For you and for me. For both of us. I wanted to take you away from here. Far away. Forever. Can you hear me, Princess?" Lila did not give a sign of life. It was no use. Boris crept back to his bed.

His suitcase, packed, stood in the hall when a nurse arrived in the morning. For days after he kept close to the house. Watching. He saw people come in and out. Nobody noticed him. And then one day the ambulance arrived. Lila was taken out on a stretcher and driven away.

It took him days to find out which hospital she was taken to. Knowing his way around hospitals it was not too difficult. He spoke to an orderly there who showed him the big bottle of after shave lotion Mandie had given him. The floor nurse received a big box of candy from her. Kept it under the counter. These two were supposed to pay particular attention to Lila and phone immediately if and when she became alert.

"How often do they visit?"

"Oh, they do not visit at all. No use for them to come. The old lady does not even know where she is."

"May I visit this patient? She is an old friend of mine."

"Sure, why not."

Boris had on his dark suit, white shirt and black tie. His Sunday best. Stopped at the Five and Ten and from the young girl behind the counter he purchased red hair ribbons.

"Princess," he whispered to Lila. No reaction. He half lifted her into a sitting position. With the hair brush he found in the drawer he started his ministrations. "My little Princess," he crooned to her, "nobody brushes your hair. Boris will do it. You will be a pretty girl like you always were — see? I brought you red ribbons. You will get double bows like you wanted before, remember?" Lila's forehead creased in a frown. She tried to bring something out from deep inside her but could not. "Princess, what did they do to you? You were so happy. My poor *Dzievochka*."

He came again next day. And every day after that. He brought her blue barrettes. With plastic pigeons on each. He brought her two purple side combs. And so it went. Day after day.

He could not bring his balalaika, he could not sing, but he whispered the songs, like before — the same songs — right into her ear. Her face showed an enormous effort. To make some sense of what was going on. But the eyes looking at him did not know who he was.

The doll Boris brought her made a strange difference. She grabbed it from his hands and would not let go. The next day the nurse told him Lila was holding on to it with all her strength. Close to her body. Crying like a baby.

With each day she became weaker and weaker. Then one day when he stepped out of the elevator, his friend, the orderly, took him aside and gave him a package. "She is gone. Your friend. The old lady died in the evening after you left. Here is the doll. She held on to it till the very end. I thought you ought to have it."

The day of the funeral Boris was at the cemetery early. In his Sunday best like always when visiting Lila. He stood among the tombstones away to the side. Not to be seen by the family. There were not many. Only a handful. Max and Joanie were there.

The coffin was lowered. Prayers and blessings intoned. Earth shovelled back, covered by wreaths and bouquets. The mourners left. And when everyone was gone, Boris approached. Out of the plastic bag he took out the doll and placed it among the flowers.